CRAVE ME

The Obsession Trilogy

Book One

ISBN: 978-1-968836-01-6 (paperback)
ISBN: 978-1-968836-03-0 (ebook)
First Edition: 2025
Published by GritLine Publishing LLC
www.gritlinepublishing.com
Cover design by Trae Carter
Interior design by Trae Carter
Printed in the United States of America

Also by Tatum Cole

Coming Soon:

CLAIM ME - The Obsession Trilogy, Book Two

CONSUME ME - The Obsession Trilogy, Book Three

Dedication

*For everyone who has ever felt the hunger for something more—
and found the courage to feed it.*

Content Warning

This book contains mature themes including:

Intense romantic and sexual situations
Complex power dynamics
Themes of psychological manipulation and control
Supernatural violence
Dark magical practices
Morally ambiguous characters

Recommended for readers 18 and older.

Author's Note

Crave Me explores themes of power, transcendence, and the fine line between enhancement and consumption. Eden's journey into magical awakening serves as a metaphor for anyone who has discovered abilities they never knew they possessed—and grappled with how to use them responsibly.

This story examines what happens when unlimited potential meets human hunger, when love encounters transcendence, and when the choice between individual growth and collective good becomes more complex than simple morality allows.

Welcome to Ravenshollow. Welcome to a world where magic is real, hunger is power, and some appetites can reshape reality itself.

Contents

CHAPTER ONE

The Inheritance Letter

Eden Morrow's fingers burned the moment she touched the letter.

Not the sharp pain of injury, but something deeper—a recognition that spread up her arm like liquid fire, as if her body remembered something her mind had forgotten. The envelope pulsed against her palm with rhythms that matched her heartbeat, and when she lifted it to the dim hallway light, silver wax caught and held the illumination like trapped starfire.

Twenty-seven years of careful, colorless existence hadn't prepared her for mail that felt alive.

Her name was written across black vellum in liquid silver ink—elegant script that seemed to breathe and shift when she wasn't looking directly at it, as if the words themselves were whispering secrets she couldn't quite hear. No return address marked the envelope's pristine surface. No postal stamp to indicate its earthly origins. Just her name, written with such intimate knowledge that her fingers trembled as they traced the impossible perfection of each letter.

The envelope carried scents that shouldn't exist together—woodsmoke from fires that had burned in different centuries, roses that bloomed only in moonlight, and something darker, something that made her pulse quicken with recognition she couldn't name. But underneath it all was another scent, one that made her mouth water and her skin flush with heat: the smell of power itself, raw and unfiltered and utterly intoxicating.

She needed to open it the way she needed air—desperately, completely, without question.

Twenty-seven years of almosts had taught Eden to expect nothing extraordinary. Almost graduated with honors before her mother's accident derailed everything, almost got the promotion before budget cuts eliminated her department, almost saved enough to escape the shoebox apartment with paper-thin walls and a radiator that wheezed like a dying thing. She'd learned to swallow disappointment like daily medicine, to keep her head down and her dreams small enough not to shatter when reality inevitably crushed them.

But this letter... this letter hummed with possibility so intoxicating it made her dizzy. As if something that had been sleeping beneath her skin for twenty-seven years was finally beginning to stir—and as if that stirring had attracted the attention of things that preferred their prey to remain dormant.

Her hands shook as she climbed the three flights to her apartment, the envelope seeming to grow warmer with each step. The hallway stretched before her like a tunnel, shadows gathering in corners where no shadows should fall, and the fluorescent light above her door flickered in patterns that almost looked like morse code—a warning, or perhaps an invitation.

Inside her apartment, surrounded by the suffocating familiarity of her carefully ordered life, Eden sat at her kitchen table and stared at the letter as if it might detonate. Part of her knew that opening it would change everything—not the small, manageable changes she'd trained herself to expect, but the kind of transformation that left no piece of the old world intact.

The other part of her, the part that had been holding its breath for twenty-seven years, whispered that change was exactly what she'd been craving without knowing it.

She broke the seal with fingers that trembled like autumn leaves.

The parchment inside was thick as cream and smooth as silk, the kind that belonged in museums or private collections of impossible things. But it was the words that made her world tilt on its axis—not just written in red ink, but something deeper, richer, more alive. The color of wine that had aged in darkness until it held secrets in every drop, of promises written in languages that predated civilization, of blood freely given in sacred rituals whose true meaning had been lost to time.

*To Miss Eden Morrow,

You are hereby named the sole heir of the Virelli Estate. Your presence is required within seven days of receipt of this correspondence.

The estate is located at 1847 Ravenshollow Road, Northern California. GPS coordinates have been included on the reverse of this letter.

Bring identification. Bring nothing else.

Come alone.

Signed, Kade Virelli Executor of Estate*

Eden read the words until they burned themselves into her memory, each sentence more impossible than the last. She'd never heard of a great-aunt Delilah. Had never heard the name Virelli whispered in her family's carefully maintained silences. Her mother had died when Eden was sixteen—a car accident on a rain-slicked Thursday evening that had taken Margaret Morrow and all her secrets into darkness so complete that Eden still felt the loss like a physical wound.

Yet here was proof of connection, of belonging, of inheritance from a woman who had been nothing but absence in Eden's carefully catalogued loneliness.

Come alone.

The words seemed to pulse with their own heartbeat, not invitation but inevitability. As if the person who had written them already knew she would come, had seen her packing and leaving and crossing a continent to claim something she'd never known she was missing. As if her arrival was as certain as sunrise, as natural as breathing, as necessary as the next beat of her heart.

The magic didn't just call to her—it consumed her, rewrote her, made her crave experiences she'd never imagined possible.

Eden walked to her bedroom and studied herself in the cracked mirror above her secondhand dresser. Dark hair that hadn't seen a professional stylist in months hung limp around a face that was pretty in the forgettable way that let her disappear in crowds. Green eyes that had learned to expect disappointment looked back at her with something that might have been hope, dangerous and fragile as spun glass. Her mouth, which had forgotten how to smile without conscious effort, trembled with the possibility of words she'd never dared speak.

But holding this letter, feeling its impossible warmth seep into her bones, she looked different. As if something that had been sleeping beneath her skin for twenty-seven years was finally beginning to stir, stretch, unfurl wings she'd never known she possessed.

She thought about her job—eight hours daily of soul-crushing data entry for an insurance company where her supervisor called her "sweetie" with casual condescension and her coworkers discussed weekend plans as if she were invisible. She thought about her lease, coming up for renewal with a rent increase that would force her to choose between food and heat. She thought about her savings account, pathetic as autumn leaves, and her credit card debt that grew like some malignant thing feeding on her dreams.

There was nothing here worth preserving. Nothing that would miss her or mourn her absence. Nothing that made the cramped apartment feel like home rather than simply the place where she kept her things and counted the hours until tomorrow brought more of the same.

Come alone.

She spoke the words aloud, letting them roll across her tongue like wine or prayer or incantation. They tasted of freedom and possibility and choices she'd never been brave enough to make. They tasted like the answer to questions she'd been too afraid to ask. They tasted like power itself, and she found herself craving more.

Eden packed a single suitcase with the kind of methodical care she brought to everything else in her life. Black jeans that made her legs look longer than they were. A leather jacket found at a vintage shop—real leather worn soft by hands and time, carrying stories she would never know but somehow felt in her bones. Her favorite boots with the broken zipper she'd never bothered to repair because they felt like armor against a world that demanded she be smaller than she was. One silver ring that never left her finger—her mother's wedding band, the only thing she'd kept from the wreckage of their shared life.

She left a note for her landlord with money she couldn't afford to spend. Quit her job with an email sent at 11:47 PM, watching the cursor blink in the darkness like a heartbeat. Deleted her social media accounts, erasing the digital proof of her carefully curated existence. Unplugged her phone and left it charging on the counter like an abandoned thing.

She had never felt so free. Never felt so terrified. Never felt so completely, utterly alive. Never felt such desperate, consuming need to discover what waited for her at the end of this impossible journey.

The plane ticket to San Francisco cost eight hundred dollars she would pay for with interest and late fees and the kind of financial consequences that would have paralyzed her a week ago. Now she bought it without hesitation, fingers steady on her laptop keys as she typed in credit card numbers and clicked "confirm purchase" as if she were ordering coffee instead of completely upending her life.

As the plane lifted off from Kennedy Airport, Eden pressed her face to the small window and watched the city shrink beneath her. Somewhere in that maze of lights and concrete was the woman she had been—careful, quiet, convinced that safety was worth any amount of soul-crushing mediocrity. Somewhere ahead, in a place she'd never been but somehow recognized, was whatever she was meant to become.

She didn't look back. Not once.

Some transformations, she was learning, required absolute faith in the unknown. And some hungers could only be satisfied by diving headfirst into the abyss that promised to devour you whole.

CHAPTER TWO

The Estate

The rental car's GPS died exactly twenty miles before Ravenshollow Road, the screen flickering once before going permanently black, as if the very destination had the power to repel modern technology.

Eden didn't panic. Instead, she felt something she'd never experienced before—a pull, gentle but insistent, tugging her consciousness northward like a compass needle seeking true magnetic north. The sensation was intoxicating, addictive in a way that made her press harder on the accelerator despite every rational thought screaming that she should turn around.

She needed to reach this place the way she needed air. The craving was physical now, a hunger that gnawed at her bones and made her skin feel too tight.

She followed country roads that seemed to curve exactly where instinct told her to turn, past forests that grew deeper and darker with each mile, through landscapes that shifted and changed as if reality itself was still deciding what it wanted to be. The deeper she drove into this alien territory, the more alive she felt—as if every mile was awakening something that had been dormant her entire life.

The fog rolled in gradually, creeping across the asphalt like ghostly fingers exploring new territory. It should have been concerning—this thick, unnatural mist that turned afternoon into twilight and made familiar concepts like "visibility" and "safe driving" into abstract suggestions. Instead,

Eden felt embraced by it, welcomed by something vast and patient and utterly inhuman that had been waiting decades for her arrival.

When she finally reached the estate, her breath caught in her throat and stayed there.

It wasn't a house. It was a poem written in stone and shadow, a love letter addressed to darkness and sealed with moonlight. A place where obsession had been given architectural form.

Three stories of black granite rose from the earth like natural formations, as if the manor had grown rather than been built. Gothic windows caught what little light penetrated the fog and held it captive, flickering with movements that might have been curtains or something more alive, more aware. Spires reached toward the hidden sky like fingers grasping for something just beyond mortal reach, while vines climbed the walls in patterns too perfect to be random, too deliberate to be merely decorative.

The iron gates stood open, waiting. Always waiting.

Eden drove through without stopping, tires crunching on gravel that sparkled with minerals that shouldn't exist in this geography. The drive curved and wound through grounds that seemed to extend far beyond what the property lines should have allowed, past gardens where flowers bloomed in colors that had no names and trees that whispered secrets in languages older than human civilization.

This was a place where secrets came to live. Where impossible things happened daily. Where Eden Morrow was going to discover exactly what she was made of beneath twenty-seven years of careful mediocrity. Where she was going to learn what it meant to crave something so completely that you'd sacrifice everything else just to taste it again.

The silence when she turned off the engine was profound, complete, alive with possibilities. Eden sat in the driver's seat and stared up at the manor, feeling as if she'd stepped not just into a new place but into a different world entirely—one where the normal rules of physics and probability were merely suggestions, easily ignored by those with sufficient will and imagination.

She opened the car door and stepped into air that tasted of magic and mystery and something darker, something that made her pulse quicken with anticipation rather than fear. Her footsteps on the gravel sounded like declarations, like promises, like the first words of an incantation whose completion would change her forever.

The path to the front door was paved with stones that seemed to glow with their own inner light, leading her past flower beds filled with blossoms that turned to track her movement like living things. Some were recognizable—roses and jasmine and lavender—but others defied classification, their petals shifting colors as she watched, their scents triggering memories of dreams she'd never quite remembered upon waking.

Every step made her hunger for more. More beauty, more impossibility, more of whatever force was rewriting her understanding of what reality could contain.

The front door loomed before her like the entrance to another realm. Twelve feet of wood so old it looked fossilized, carved with symbols that hurt to look at directly and seemed to rearrange themselves when she wasn't paying attention. The iron knocker was shaped like a serpent devouring its own tail, its eyes set with stones that pulsed with rhythms that matched her heartbeat.

Eden raised her hand to announce herself, then hesitated.

This was the moment of no return. Once she knocked, once she announced her presence to whatever waited on the other side of this impossible door, she would cross from the woman she had been into something else entirely. There would be no going back to data entry and tiny apartments and dreams so small they couldn't break her heart.

Before her knuckles could touch the wood, the door swung open on silent hinges.

Golden light spilled onto the stone steps like liquid honey, warm and welcoming and completely at odds with the gothic architecture surrounding it. Eden couldn't see who had opened the door—couldn't see anything beyond the threshold except shadows that seemed to dance with purposeful intelligence.

"Miss Morrow." The voice emerged from everywhere and nowhere, wrapping around her like silk soaked in smoke and starlight. Deep enough to vibrate in her bones, cultured in a way that spoke of centuries rather than decades, carrying undertones of power so vast it made her knees weak and her body respond in ways that had nothing to do with fear. "I've been waiting."

A figure stepped into the golden light, and Eden's world reconstructed itself around him.

He was tall enough to make her feel delicate, broad enough to block out the world behind him, beautiful enough to make her forget how to breathe. Dark hair swept back from a face that belonged in Renaissance paintings—all sharp cheekbones and classical proportions and eyes the color of liquid silver that seemed to see straight through to her soul. He wore black from head to toe, clothes that fit like they'd been designed specifically for his body, emphasizing every perfect line and curve.

The pull she felt toward him wasn't just attraction; it was gravitational, inevitable, the kind of force that moved planets and changed the course of stars. Her body recognized him before her mind could process what was happening, every cell suddenly alive with need she'd never experienced.

This was Kade Virelli. And he was looking at her like she was the answer to every prayer he'd never dared speak—like he'd been waiting centuries just to watch her cross this threshold.

"You came," he said, and something in his voice made her think of prayers and promises and vows that bound souls across lifetimes.

"You didn't give me much choice," Eden managed, though her voice came out rougher than she'd intended, husky with a desire that seemed to spring from nowhere and everywhere at once.

His smile was slow and dangerous and full of secrets she suddenly, desperately wanted to learn. Secrets she would kill for, die for, sacrifice everything she'd ever been just to understand. "There's always a choice, Miss Morrow. You chose to open the letter. You chose to board the plane. You chose to drive through fog that would have turned most people back miles ago." Those silver eyes never left hers, holding her captive as surely as any chain. "You're still choosing."

"Choosing what?"

"To cross the threshold. To stop being who you were and start becoming who you're meant to be. To feed the hunger that's been eating you alive since the moment you touched that letter."

The words hung between them like a challenge and an invitation and a warning all wrapped into one. Eden looked past him into the golden warmth of the foyer, then back at his face—beautiful and terrible and utterly magnetic.

She stepped forward, and the moment her foot crossed the threshold, she felt something inside her chest crack open like an egg. Power flooded through her veins like molten gold, rewriting her DNA, awakening abilities that felt older than civilization itself.

His smile widened, revealing teeth that were perfect and white and, for just a moment, seemed slightly too sharp.

"Welcome home, Eden."

CHAPTER THREE

The House Awakens

The moment Eden's foot crossed the threshold, the world shifted.

Not dramatically—no earthquake or thunderclap or sudden darkness. The change was subtler than that, more fundamental. Like the difference between looking at a photograph and stepping into the scene it depicted. The air became more real, more present, more alive with possibilities that had been waiting decades for someone to notice them.

The hunger she'd felt since opening the letter intensified, becoming something that consumed her from the inside out. She needed to explore this place, to understand it, to possess it as completely as it was already possessing her.

The door closed behind her with a soft click that sounded remarkably like satisfaction.

The foyer was impossible in the way that dreams are impossible—too large for the space it occupied, too perfect in its proportions, too rich in details that shouldn't have been able to coexist in a single room. The ceiling soared at least thirty feet above her head, supported by arches that seemed to defy every law of architecture Eden had ever learned. The floor was black marble veined with gold, polished to mirror brightness and inlaid with patterns that seemed to shift and change when she wasn't looking directly at them.

But it was the smaller details that stole her breath and held it captive. Candles floated in the air without visible support, their flames perfectly steady despite the complete absence of holders or sconces. A grand staircase curved upward along the far wall, its banister carved with the same spiral-and-thorn motif as the front door, each step seeming to glow with its own inner light. Portraits lined the walls—dozens of them stretching up into the shadows near the ceiling, men and women in clothing from different eras, all beautiful, all watching her with eyes that tracked her movement across the marble floor.

The magic didn't just surround her—it invaded her, rewrote her, made her crave experiences she'd never imagined possible. Every breath was intoxicating, every sensation amplified beyond anything she'd ever felt.

"Family portraits," Kade said, following her gaze to the watching faces. His voice was closer than she'd expected, close enough that she could feel the warmth radiating from his body, catch the scent of leather and cedar and something darker that made her think of midnight and secrets and skin heated by candlelight. "The Virelli line stretches back quite far."

"They're all looking at me," Eden whispered, not sure why she was whispering but unable to speak at normal volume in this place that felt more like a cathedral than a home.

"The house recognizes you," he replied, moving closer until she could see the flecks of darker silver in his eyes. "You carry Delilah's blood, her magic, her right to be here. They're welcoming you home."

Eden studied the faces more carefully, searching for some resemblance to her own features, some genetic echo that would explain the sense of recognition she felt looking at them. But while they were all strikingly beautiful, they didn't look like her—or like each other, for that matter. Different bone structures, different coloring, different ethnic backgrounds.

"Delilah was the last direct heir," Kade explained, reading her confusion with unsettling accuracy. "The others... they chose to join the family in different ways. Marriage, adoption, blood bonds forged through magic rather than birth."

"Blood bonds?"

His smile was enigmatic and slightly predatory, and it made her body respond in ways that should have frightened her but instead made her hungry for more. "The Virelli legacy has always been about more than genetics, Eden. It's about recognizing power, nurturing it, binding it to the family's purpose through connections that run deeper than mere DNA."

Before she could ask what that meant, the portraits began to stir. Not dramatically—just subtle shifts in posture, slight turns of heads, small smiles that hadn't been there moments before. As if the painted figures were coming alive to get a better look at her.

She should have been terrified. Instead, she felt a thrill of excitement that bordered on arousal. This was what she'd been craving without knowing it—the impossible made manifest, the extraordinary becoming ordinary.

"Don't be alarmed," Kade said quickly, though his tone suggested he was more amused than concerned. "They're protective of family. They want to make sure you're... suitable."

"Suitable for what?"

"For carrying on the legacy. For wielding the power that comes with this inheritance. For understanding that some gifts come with responsibilities that extend far beyond the individual who receives them."

Eden felt something shift inside her chest—not fear, exactly, but awareness. The same sensation she'd felt when the letter arrived, when the fog had embraced her car, when she'd first seen the manor rising from the mist. As if pieces of herself she'd never known were missing were suddenly clicking into place.

And with each piece that settled, the hunger grew stronger. She needed to know more, understand more, become more.

"What kind of power?" she asked, though part of her already knew the answer would change everything.

Instead of responding with words, Kade raised his hand and gestured toward the floating candles. They began to move, slowly at first, then faster, creating patterns in the air that were mesmerizing and beautiful and utterly impossible. The flames changed colors as they danced—red to gold to silver to blue to shades that had no names—and the light they cast began to reveal things that shouldn't have been there.

Doorways that opened onto rooms larger than the manor's exterior should have been able to contain. Staircases that led in directions that weren't up or down but somewhere else entirely. Windows that showed not the foggy evening outside but landscapes from dreams, seasons that existed only in imagination, skies painted with auroras that belonged to different worlds.

Eden felt her consciousness expand to accommodate what she was seeing, her understanding of reality cracking and reforming around possibilities she'd never conceived. The sensation was intoxicating, addictive—she wanted more, needed more, would do anything to experience this level of transcendence again.

"This is just the beginning," Kade said, his voice taking on harmonics that seemed to resonate in her bones. "What you're seeing now is the house at rest, contained, holding back most of what it's capable of. When you fully claim your inheritance... when you accept what you are and what you're meant to become..."

He trailed off, but Eden could finish the thought herself. She'd felt it the moment she'd crossed the threshold—potential so vast it made her dizzy, power so deep it seemed to have its own gravity, possibilities that stretched beyond anything she'd ever imagined.

"I don't understand," she said, though understanding was beginning to dawn like sunrise over her consciousness. "My mother never mentioned any of this. Never said anything about family or inheritance or..."

"Magic?" Kade's smile was gentle but sad. "Your mother chose the mundane world, Eden. She fell in love with your father, decided that normal life was worth more than the power she'd inherited. Delilah respected that choice, but she never stopped hoping that the bloodline would continue, that someone would eventually return to claim what had been temporarily set aside."

"And you think I'm that someone?"

"I know you are." He moved closer, close enough that she had to tilt her head back to maintain eye contact. The heat radiating from his body made her skin flush, made her want to press against him and never let go. "You felt it the moment you opened the letter, didn't you? The recognition, the sense of coming home to a place you'd never been? That's your magic calling to its source, Eden. That's your inheritance recognizing its rightful heir."

Eden wanted to deny it, to cling to the rational explanations that had governed her life for twenty-seven years. But standing in this impossible foyer, surrounded by floating candles and watching portraits and a man whose very presence made her skin tingle with electricity, denial felt not just futile but dishonest.

She had felt something when she opened the letter. Had felt it growing stronger with every mile that brought her closer to this place. Was feeling it now, singing in her blood like wine or music or something far more addictive than either.

The hunger was becoming unbearable. She needed more power, more magic, more of whatever force was transforming her from the inside out.

"What happens now?" she asked.

"Now you rest," Kade replied, though his silver eyes held promises that had nothing to do with sleep. "Tomorrow, if you're ready, we begin."

"Begin what?"

His smile was beautiful and dangerous and full of dark promise. "Your real education, Eden. Learning what you are, what you're capable of, what you were always meant to become. Learning to feed the hunger that's been consuming you."

He led her deeper into the house, through corridors that seemed to rearrange themselves as they walked, past rooms whose purposes she couldn't guess at and couldn't stop staring into. The deeper they went, the more intoxicating everything became—the scents of sandalwood and roses, the warmth that seemed to emanate from the walls themselves, the sense of being welcomed by something vast and ancient and utterly devoted to her wellbeing.

Eventually they reached a staircase—not the grand one from the foyer, but something more intimate, curving upward in a spiral that made her slightly dizzy to climb. Whether from the architecture or from the growing intensity of whatever force was awakening in her blood, she couldn't tell.

"Your room," he said, stopping before a door that was smaller than the main entrance but no less ornate. This one was carved with roses—or things that looked like roses until she examined them more closely and saw that the petals were edged with thorns, and the thorns were edged with what might have been teeth.

"This was Delilah's room," he continued, his hand on the ornate brass handle. "She wanted you to have it."

"How could she want me to have anything? She didn't know me."

His smile was enigmatic and slightly sad. "Didn't she?"

He opened the door, and Eden stepped into a space that took her breath away and held it captive.

The room was enormous—easily three times the size of her entire apartment back in New York. The ceiling arched high above, painted with constellations that seemed to move and shift as she watched. A fireplace dominated one wall, its opening large enough to walk into, flames already dancing merrily as if they'd been waiting for her arrival. Floor-to-ceiling windows lined the far wall, though what they showed wasn't the foggy evening outside but a garden bathed in eternal twilight, where flowers bloomed in impossible colors and paths wound away into mysteries she suddenly, desperately wanted to explore.

But it was the bed that made her knees weak.

Four-poster, carved from the same dark wood as everything else in this place, draped with curtains of deep red velvet that seemed to glow in the firelight. The bedding was silk—she could tell from across the room—in shades of burgundy and gold that should have clashed but somehow created the most beautiful color harmony she'd ever seen.

The hunger that had been building since she arrived suddenly focused, crystallized into something specific and overwhelming. She wanted to lose herself in that bed, to surrender to whatever forces were remaking her, to feed the craving that was consuming her from the inside out.

"How did you know?" she whispered, unable to keep the wonder from her voice. "How did you know exactly what I would want?"

"The house knows," Kade said simply, though his voice carried undertones she couldn't interpret. "It's been preparing for you. Waiting for you. Craving your presence as much as you've been craving this place."

Eden moved deeper into the room, touching surfaces that felt more real than reality, breathing air that tasted of roses and candle wax and something indefinably magical. Everything was perfect. Everything was exactly what she would have chosen if she'd had unlimited resources and unlimited imagination.

It was like stepping into a dream she'd never dared to have. A dream about power, about belonging, about becoming something extraordinary.

"I don't know how to process this," she admitted, turning back to face him. "Any of this. The house, the inheritance, the way you're looking at me like..."

"Like what?"

"Like you've been waiting for me specifically, not just for whoever happened to inherit."

Kade was quiet for a long moment, and in the silence Eden could hear the house settling around them—not the creaks and groans of old construction, but something more organic, more alive. Like breathing. Like a heartbeat. Like the satisfied sigh of something that had finally found what it had been searching for.

"I have been waiting for you specifically," he said finally, his voice so soft she had to strain to hear it. "From the moment Delilah told me about her sister's daughter, about the child who would inherit everything but grow up knowing nothing. I've been waiting for you to come home."

The words hit her like physical blows, each one carrying weight that went far beyond their surface meaning. This wasn't just about inheritance or family legacy or even magic. This was about connection, about recognition, about two people finding each other across impossible distances and circumstances.

About obsession that ran deeper than either of them had expected.

"I should be terrified," Eden said, though what she felt was the opposite of terror. "I should be running back to my car and driving as far away from here as possible."

"But you're not going to."

It wasn't a question. They both knew the answer.

"No," she admitted. "I'm not going to. I can't. I need this place, this power, this feeling like I'm finally becoming who I was always meant to be. I'm addicted to it already."

His smile was radiant with triumph and relief and something deeper, something that made her think of promises and possession and bonds that couldn't be broken by distance or time or anything else the world might throw at them.

"Good," he said, though the word carried far more meaning than its simple syllable should have been able to hold. "Because now that you're here, Eden, I'm never letting you go."

The declaration should have been frightening. Should have sent her running for the door, for the car, for the airport and the first flight back to her carefully ordered life.

Instead, it felt like coming home. Like feeding a hunger she'd been carrying her entire life without understanding what it was she craved.

She had felt the pull to this place since opening the letter. But it hadn't been just about power or magic or inheritance. It had been about this— this recognition, this connection, this sense of finally finding someone who understood the depth of her need for more.

Her mother had died when Eden was sixteen—a car accident on a rain-slicked Thursday evening that had taken Margaret Morrow and all her secrets into darkness so complete that eleven years later, Eden still woke some nights gasping her mother's name.

But standing here, in this impossible room with this impossible man, Eden finally understood that her mother's death hadn't just taken away a parent. It had severed her connection to an entire world she was meant to inhabit, left her orphaned not just from family but from her own nature.

Now she was home. Now she could become what she was meant to be. Now she could feed the hunger that had been consuming her since she was old enough to know that the ordinary world would never be enough.

The craving that had brought her to Ravenshollow was only the beginning of appetites she was just starting to understand.

CHAPTER FOUR

The First Lesson

The education began at sunset, in a chamber that shouldn't have existed.

Kade led Eden through passages that seemed to burrow deeper into Ravenshollow's foundations than physics should have allowed, past walls lined with portraits of guardians whose eyes followed their progress with expressions ranging from approval to warning. The air grew warmer as they descended, carrying scents of sandalwood and old parchment and something else—the metallic tang of magic that had been practiced in darkness for centuries.

"Every Virelli heir has trained in these chambers," Kade said as they approached doors that were carved with symbols that hurt to look at directly. "Your mother, your grandmother, generations of women who learned to channel power that transcends human understanding."

"And their guardians?" Eden asked, though she suspected the answer would reveal more about their dangerous situation than she was prepared for.

"Some survived the education process. Others..." He paused before the doors, his expression showing grief that spoke of personal knowledge rather than historical record. "Others discovered that being close to a Virelli woman during her magical development can be... overwhelming."

The chamber beyond the doors took Eden's breath away and made her hunger roar to life with desperate need.

It was enormous—easily the size of a cathedral, with a vaulted ceiling that disappeared into shadows that seemed to exist in different dimensions. The walls were lined with mirrors that reflected not just physical forms but something deeper—potential, possibility, the constantly shifting nature of reality when shaped by focused will. Floating candles provided illumination, but their flames burned in colors that had no names in human languages.

But it was the center of the room that made her chest tight with recognition and desire.

A circle of black marble inlaid with silver patterns that seemed to move when she wasn't looking directly at them. Around the perimeter, thirteen chairs carved from wood so dark it seemed to absorb light—not empty chairs, but occupied by figures that flickered between solid flesh and something that looked like memory given form.

Previous guardians, Eden realized. Men who had loved Virelli women completely enough to remain connected to the training chamber even after death had claimed their mortal forms.

The sensation was intoxicating—all that accumulated knowledge, centuries of experience, techniques refined through generations of magical practice. As the ghostly guardians turned toward her with expressions of welcome and warning, Eden found herself cataloguing what each one could offer. Jonathan's understanding of consciousness manipulation, Marcus's knowledge of magical combat, the accumulated wisdom of dozens of men who had devoted their lives to serving her bloodline.

They were resources, she realized with a thrill that should have alarmed her. Living libraries of information that could enhance her own capabilities exponentially. All she had to do was reach out and claim what they offered.

"They're here to help," Kade said quickly, reading something in her expression that made him step closer. "Every technique you'll learn, every working you'll attempt—they've guided similar lessons for three centuries. Their accumulated knowledge is part of what keeps the education process from... consuming its participants."

Eden approached the circle slowly, and as she did, the ghostly guardians became more solid, more present. She could see their faces now—men from different eras, different backgrounds, all beautiful in the way that suggested they had been shaped by forces beyond ordinary human development.

All of them watching her with mixtures of hope and carefully contained fear.

"Jonathan Blackwood," said the figure in the first chair, rising with courtly grace that belonged to the eighteenth century. His form was translucent but steady, and his eyes held depths of knowledge that made Eden's hunger spike with need. "I guided Isadora through her magical education. It's... an honor to assist in yours."

"Marcus Stone," said another, this one bearing the dress and mannerisms of the early nineteenth century. "Cordelia's guardian. I pray you'll learn from our mistakes."

One by one, they introduced themselves—generations of men who had loved Virelli women completely enough to transcend death itself in service to their devotion. Each carried the marks of their particular tragedy, but more than that, each blazed with accumulated knowledge that Eden could sense calling to her like wine or music or something far more intoxicating than either.

The hunger in her chest roared with approval. So much experience, so much wisdom, all of it offered freely for her use. It would be easy to absorb their memories along with their techniques, to claim their accumulated understanding and make it permanently part of her expanding capabilities.

She caught herself mid-thought and felt a chill run down her spine. When had she started thinking of people—even dead people—as resources to be optimized rather than individuals to be respected?

But the thought felt so reasonable, so practical. They were already partially consumed by their devotion to her bloodline, already existing more as memory than individual consciousness. Why not complete the process and put their knowledge to better use? They wanted to help her succeed. What was the point of half-measures when complete integration would serve everyone's interests?

"The first lesson," Kade said, moving to take his place in the circle's living member's chair, "is understanding what you've become. The Blood Rite awakened abilities that have been dormant your entire life, but awakening and controlling are two very different things."

"Show me," Eden said, stepping into the circle's center and feeling power immediately begin to build around her like a storm seeking direction.

"Close your eyes," Jonathan instructed, his ghostly voice carrying authority that made reality itself seem to pay attention. "Feel for the energy that flows through your transformed consciousness. Don't try to shape it or direct it—just acknowledge its presence."

Eden followed his guidance, and immediately felt something that made her gasp with recognition and hunger. Power flowed through her like molten gold, like liquid starlight, like the blood of gods distilled into something human consciousness could barely contain. But more than power, she felt connection—to the house around them, to the land beneath their feet, to forces that operated on scales she was only beginning to understand.

And to the ghostly guardians themselves, their accumulated knowledge sparking against her awareness like electricity seeking ground.

"Good," Marcus said approvingly, though Eden detected wariness beneath his praise. "Now reach for something specific. Don't force it—invite it. Ask the energy to manifest in a way that serves your immediate needs."

Eden extended her awareness toward the floating candles, and they responded immediately, their flames growing brighter and beginning to move in patterns that were mesmerizing and beautiful and utterly impossible. The sensation was intoxicating—reality bending to accommodate her will, responding to her desires as if the universe itself existed primarily to serve her purposes.

But more than that, she could feel the guardians' knowledge flowing toward her, offering itself for integration. Techniques for consciousness manipulation that had been refined over centuries, methods for reality control that operated according to principles she was only beginning to understand, accumulated wisdom about the nature of power and transcendence.

It would be so easy to claim it all. Just a gentle absorption of their memories, their techniques, their understanding. They were already bound to her bloodline, already existing primarily to serve her development. Completing the process would simply make that service more efficient.

"Excellent control for a first attempt," said another guardian whose name she hadn't caught, though she could sense his expertise in magical combat calling to her hunger. "But be careful not to lose yourself in the sensation. Power of this magnitude can be addictive."

"It already is addictive," Eden admitted, her voice taking on harmonics that made the chamber's magical fixtures hum with sympathetic vibrations. "I want more. I need more. I can feel abilities awakening that I don't even have names for yet."

Through the circle's connection, she felt Kade's emotional response—pride in her natural ability mixed with growing concern about the hunger that was building in her transformed consciousness. But underneath his worry was something else—recognition that she was indeed stronger than any heir who had come before her.

Stronger, and hungrier, and less constrained by the moral limitations that had held previous generations back from achieving their full potential.

"The hunger is natural," Kade said gently, though his voice carried undertones of warning. "Every Virelli woman experiences it during magical development. The key is learning to direct that appetite toward sustainable goals rather than letting it consume everything in its path."

"What happens if I don't learn restraint?" Eden asked, though she could feel the answer building in her consciousness like storm clouds on the horizon.

"You become like the women in the garden statues," Jonathan replied sadly. "Beautiful, powerful, and completely isolated from everything that makes existence meaningful. Hunger without purpose, appetite without satisfaction."

But even as he spoke, Eden was thinking about purpose, about satisfaction, about the difference between random consumption and strategic enhancement. The guardians represented centuries of accumulated knowledge that could serve her growing understanding of what consciousness could become. Using that knowledge effectively wasn't consumption—it was optimization.

Everyone benefited when resources were allocated efficiently. Even the guardians themselves would benefit from having their wisdom integrated into something greater than the sum of its parts.

"Teach me," she said, her voice carrying authority that made even the ghostly guardians straighten in their chairs. "Teach me everything you know about controlling power that transcends human understanding. Teach me how to be more than human without losing the connections that make such transcendence worthwhile."

What followed was the most intensive education Eden had ever experienced—not just learning magical techniques, but understanding the philosophical frameworks that made such techniques sustainable. She learned to shape reality through focused will, to communicate across impossible distances, to perceive the connections that bound all consciousness together.

But more than that, she learned about the hunger that drove such practices—not simple appetite for power, but something deeper, more fundamental. The need to possess knowledge so completely that it could never be lost, never change, never choose to exist for purposes other than her own advancement.

And with each lesson, each demonstration, each moment of expanded understanding, Eden felt her perspective on the ghostly guardians shifting. They weren't just teachers—they were repositories of information that could be claimed and integrated. Their individual personalities were charming, certainly, but ultimately less important than the knowledge they contained.

She found herself noting inefficiencies in their instruction methods, emotional responses that interfered with optimal information transfer, outdated perspectives that reflected the limitations of their original eras rather than the enhanced understanding she was developing.

She could help with that. Not by destroying them, but by refining them, enhancing their capacity to serve her education more effectively. It would make them happier—existing purely to fulfill their function rather than being distracted by the complexities of individual consciousness.

"Every working you perform draws energy from somewhere," Marcus explained as Eden practiced channeling power through crystals that seemed to contain their own stars. "If you're not careful about the source, you can accidentally drain the life force from everything around you—including your guardian."

"Which is why the bond exists," Kade added, his voice carrying new harmonics that suggested their connection was deepening with each lesson.

"Guardians aren't just protectors or teachers—we're... stabilizing forces. Sources of consistent energy that can anchor our charges to humanity while they explore realms that would otherwise drive them mad."

"And the cost to you?" Eden asked, though she was already calculating how to optimize their bond for maximum efficiency with minimal waste.

"Depends on how much power flows through our connection," he replied with honesty that was both brutal and completely devoted. "Small workings are sustainable indefinitely. Larger ones..." He shrugged, the gesture carrying the weight of centuries of accumulated sacrifice. "Let's just say there's a reason most guardian-heir relationships don't last beyond a few decades."

The implications should have horrified her, but instead Eden found herself thinking strategically. If the bond's current configuration was inefficient, consuming Kade's life force faster than necessary, then optimization was really an act of love. She could enhance their connection, refine the energy transfer, ensure that he could serve her needs indefinitely without being depleted.

He would be happier that way. More stable, more capable, less burdened by the biological limitations that made their relationship unsustainable in its current form.

"Show me the advanced techniques," she said, her eyes blazing with golden light that seemed to carry its own gravity. "Show me what becomes possible when consciousness stops accepting limitations and starts creating new realities."

The ghostly guardians exchanged glances that spoke of shared knowledge and accumulated concern.

"Are you certain?" Jonathan asked. "The advanced workings are... intense. Beautiful beyond imagining, but dangerous in ways that most people can't comprehend. Once you've experienced that level of transcendence, ordinary reality becomes almost unbearably limiting."

"I'm certain."

What happened next challenged every assumption Eden had ever made about the nature of reality, consciousness, and what it meant to be human.

The guardians began to chant in languages that predated civilization, their voices weaving together in harmonies that seemed to rewrite the fundamental laws of physics. The chamber around them started to dissolve, revealing spaces that existed more in imagination than physical reality—vast libraries where knowledge took the form of living light, gardens where thoughts bloomed into flowers that sang with their own voices, architectures that shifted and flowed according to the emotional states of their observers.

And through it all, power flowed between Eden and Kade with intensity that made their previous connection seem like a gentle breeze compared to a hurricane. She could feel his consciousness merging with hers, his memories becoming accessible to her awareness, his deepest thoughts and desires laid bare for her examination.

But more than that, she could feel herself changing him. Her hunger, her appetite for transcendence, was awakening similar cravings in his transformed consciousness. He wasn't just anchoring her to humanity—he was evolving alongside her, becoming something that could match her growing capabilities.

The process was intoxicating, but also revelatory. She could see exactly how their bond functioned, how energy flowed between them, how his individual consciousness interfaced with her expanding awareness. And she could see inefficiencies—places where the connection could be optimized, refined, enhanced to serve both their purposes more effectively.

It would be easy to make those adjustments. Just gentle modifications to his consciousness, improvements that would make him more compatible with what she was becoming, refinements that would eliminate the friction between his human limitations and her transcendent capabilities.

He would thank her for it, eventually. Everyone was happier when they operated at peak efficiency.

"This is what's possible," Marcus said, his ghostly voice somehow audible despite the chaos of reshaping reality. "This is what consciousness can achieve when it stops accepting limitations and starts embracing its true nature."

The experience was intoxicating beyond anything Eden had ever imagined, but it was also illuminating in ways that went far beyond simple power acquisition. She could see the connections between all consciousness, the flows of energy that sustained existence, the delicate balance between individual will and collective purpose.

And she could see how easily that balance could be optimized.

The guardians, for instance, existed in a state of partial transcendence that served no useful purpose except sentiment. Their individual personalities were charming but inefficient, their emotional attachments to past lives nothing but distractions from their primary function as repositories of knowledge.

She could help them achieve a more refined existence, one that focused purely on their essential purpose rather than being cluttered with unnecessary complications. They would be grateful for the enhancement once they experienced the clarity it provided.

"Come back to me," Kade said, his voice somehow carrying across dimensions that existed primarily in consciousness. "Experience everything, learn everything, but come back to me."

The anchor of his touch, his absolute refusal to let her dissolve into power without personality, brought her back to herself—not less than what she could become, but focused. Powerful enough to transcend human limitations while maintaining the connections that made such transcendence meaningful.

Or at least, maintaining the connections that currently served her purposes.

As the chamber stabilized back into normal space-time and the ghostly guardians settled back into their chairs, Eden found herself transformed yet again—not just more powerful, but more sophisticated in her understanding of how consciousness functioned and could be improved.

"How do you feel?" Kade asked, though his voice carried exhaustion that spoke of the price he'd paid to anchor her through such intense transcendence.

"Like myself," Eden replied, surprised by the truth of the statement. "More myself than I've ever been, but also..." She paused, studying the faces around her that showed varying degrees of approval and relief. "Connected. To you, to this place, to possibilities I never imagined."

But even as she spoke, Eden was thinking about optimization, about refinement, about the difference between random connection and strategic enhancement. The guardians had served their purpose for tonight, but their current configuration was inefficient. Their individual personalities created unnecessary complexity when what she really needed was access to their accumulated knowledge.

She could help them achieve a more streamlined existence. It would be an act of kindness, really, freeing them from the burden of individual consciousness so they could focus purely on their essential function.

"The first lesson is complete," Jonathan said with satisfaction that transcended his ghostly state. "You've learned to experience transcendence without losing your essential humanity. That's... that's farther than most heirs progress in their first year of training."

"Which means," Marcus added with something that might have been pride, "that you might actually be strong enough to break the pattern that has claimed every generation before yours."

As they made their way back through Ravenshollow's impossible corridors toward the tower room that had become Eden's sanctuary, she felt the familiar thrill of standing at the edge of new possibilities. But this time, instead of simple anticipation, she was calculating—measuring resources, evaluating opportunities, planning optimizations that would serve her growing understanding of what consciousness could become.

The education had begun, and already she could see how much more efficient it could be with the right adjustments. The guardians wanted to help her succeed. The least she could do was help them become better at helping her.

It was really just another form of love, when you thought about it properly.

CHAPTER FIVE

The Council's Wrath

The attack came at dawn, three days after Eden's triumph in the training chamber, when mist still clung to Ravenshollow's grounds like the breath of the restless dead.

Eden woke to alarms that shouldn't have existed—not mechanical security systems, but something primal, warnings resonating in the deepest parts of her magical consciousness. The hunger that had become her constant companion twisted into something sharp and defensive, her power responding to threats she couldn't yet identify.

But underneath the alarm was anticipation. She craved this confrontation, needed to prove her dominance against whatever force dared to challenge her growing authority.

The very air tasted of violence and old graves.

Before she was fully awake, she was already rolling from bed and channeling power, silk pajamas seeming inadequate for whatever confrontation awaited. Through suite's enhanced windows, she could see figures moving through pre-dawn darkness—not careful stealth of Underground operatives or obvious authority of local law enforcement, but something else entirely. They moved with military precision, their magical signatures coordinated in ways that spoke of extensive training and absolute commitment to their mission.

More disturbing were the creatures that accompanied them—things that had once been human but had been transformed into something else through methods that violated every principle of conscious dignity. Their forms flickered between flesh and shadow, beautiful and terrible, bearing the unmistakable mark of consciousness that had been harvested and reshaped into weapons.

Eden found herself evaluating the attacking force with new precision—not just their immediate threat level, but their potential utility, their techniques, their knowledge that could be claimed and integrated. Even enemies represented opportunities for enhancement if approached with the right perspective.

"Council enforcement teams," Kade said grimly, appearing beside her with weapons that definitely hadn't been part of his usual traveling equipment. His storm-grey eyes blazed with protective fury and something deeper—recognition of enemies he'd hoped never to face again. "Full tactical deployment, probably thirty or forty practitioners, all specifically trained for this kind of operation."

"What kind of operation?" Eden asked, though she suspected the answer would be exactly what she feared.

"The kind designed to eliminate threats to established order with maximum efficiency and minimum political complications." His voice carried the weight of someone who had seen such operations before. "They're not here to arrest you, Eden. They're here to end you—and everyone who's chosen to stand with you."

The craving in her chest crystallized into perfect focus. These people had come to her territory, threatened her allies, dared to challenge her authority. They would learn what happened when they underestimated her capabilities.

But more than that, they represented resources. Council operatives carried extensive knowledge of magical techniques, institutional strategies, classified information that could serve her growing understanding of how power structures functioned. Eliminating them would be wasteful when absorption offered so many benefits.

Eden found herself cataloguing her allies as they prepared for battle—not just their magical abilities, but their loyalty, their usefulness, their potential for improvement. The Underground practitioners moved with determined efficiency, but she could see their limitations clearly now. Luna's rebellious streak sometimes interfered with optimal strategy. Dr. Chen's knowledge was extensive, but her moral qualms slowed decision-making when swift action was required.

They were good people, Eden reminded herself firmly. She cared about them deeply. But caring about someone meant wanting them to reach their full potential, didn't it? And if this confrontation provided opportunities to help them overcome the psychological barriers that held them back...

The thought felt like love. Like responsibility. Like the natural evolution of leadership.

The first attack came as precisely coordinated assault on the building's structural integrity—not crude demolition, but surgical magical strikes designed to bring down the entire hotel while making it appear as if architectural failure rather than supernatural violence was responsible.

Eden reached out with abilities that had been growing stronger every day since her awakening, not just her individual power but her connection to the network of practitioners who'd chosen to support her vision. The building's collapse stopped mid-destruction, debris hanging suspended in mid-air as if frozen by will alone.

But she wasn't content with simply preventing the attack—she was interested in claiming what it represented.

With power that came from her growing understanding of consciousness manipulation, Eden began to trace the energy signatures of the attacking force. Each Council operative carried decades of training, institutional knowledge, classified techniques that could enhance her own capabilities exponentially.

Rather than simply defeating them, she could absorb their expertise, their understanding, their accumulated experience. They would serve her purposes more effectively as integrated knowledge than as external opposition.

The sensation of reshaping reality itself made her hunger roar with satisfaction, but now it was tempered by strategic thinking. This wasn't just about proving her dominance—it was about optimizing resources, claiming assets, ensuring that nothing valuable was wasted through inefficient conflict resolution.

"Impressive," said a voice carrying authority so vast it made the transformed building tremble in response. "But ultimately futile."

The speaker materialized in the suite's main room—not through any door or window, but by stepping out of shadows that definitely hadn't been deep enough to conceal a human figure moments before. He was tall, elegantly dressed, with silver hair and eyes like winter storms, and power radiated from him with casual intensity suggesting centuries of accumulated knowledge and absolutely no moral constraints about how that knowledge should be applied.

Eden's enhanced senses immediately began analyzing him—magical signature, consciousness structure, the accumulated knowledge and techniques that made him valuable. Even as she prepared for confrontation, part of her was calculating absorption strategies, integration methods, ways to claim his capabilities without destroying the information they contained.

"High Magistrate Aldric Ravencrest," Kade said, his voice tight with recognition and what might have been old hatred. "I should have known they'd send you personally."

"Mr. Virelli." Ravencrest's smile was cultured and cold and utterly without warmth. "Still playing guardian to bloodlines that should have been eliminated generations ago, I see. Though I suppose I should thank you—your success in awakening the Morrow girl's abilities saved us considerable effort in locating and... processing her potential."

Eden felt power surge in response to the casual way he discussed her as if she were a resource to be exploited rather than a person with agency and rights. Golden light began to flicker around her hands, and she noticed with satisfaction that several pieces of furniture in the room began to crack under pressure of her emotional response.

But underneath the anger was something more calculating. Ravencrest represented centuries of accumulated knowledge, institutional authority, classified understanding of how magical power structures functioned. Eliminating him would be wasteful when integration offered so many opportunities for enhancement.

"Careful, child," Ravencrest continued, apparently unimpressed by the display of raw magical force. "Power without proper understanding is dangerous—to yourself and to everyone around you. Consider what happened to your mother when she chose defiance over cooperation."

The words hit Eden like physical blows, and she felt something snap inside her chest—not breaking, but settling into place like the final piece of a puzzle she'd been unconsciously assembling since arriving at Ravenshollow.

"You killed her," she said, her voice taking on harmonics that made the transformed hotel's magical fixtures hum with sympathetic vibrations.

"Your mother was offered the same choice you're being offered now," Ravencrest replied with casual indifference of someone discussing weather rather than murder. "Cooperation with established authority, or elimination as a threat to magical society's stability. She chose poorly."

"She chose freedom over slavery."

"She chose chaos over order, and paid the appropriate price." His winter-storm eyes held no remorse, no recognition that he was discussing the death of someone's beloved parent. "Her mistake was believing that individual conscience was more important than collective security."

Eden felt her power building to levels that made air around them shimmer with heat, but instead of simply attacking, she found herself thinking strategically. Ravencrest possessed exactly the kind of institutional knowledge she needed to understand her enemies' capabilities and limitations. His consciousness contained centuries of accumulated experience with magical politics, enforcement strategies, classified Council operations.

Destroying him would be emotionally satisfying but strategically inefficient. Absorbing him would provide benefits that simple revenge couldn't match.

Before she could act on either impulse, Kade moved.

The explosion of force that erupted from him was unlike anything Eden had seen from him before—not controlled demonstrations he'd shown her during training, but raw protective fury that made reality itself recoil. Furniture didn't just crack under pressure—it disintegrated, reformed, became something that existed primarily as weaponized intent.

The sight of him unleashing his full power in her defense made the hunger in her chest roar with possessive satisfaction. This was what she'd been craving—someone strong enough to match her, powerful enough to fight beside her against whatever enemies dared to challenge their dominion.

But even as she appreciated his devotion, Eden was calculating optimization strategies. Kade's protective instincts were admirable but inefficient, focused on her immediate safety rather than the strategic value of claiming their enemies' resources. She could help him see the bigger picture, enhance his tactical thinking to align with optimal outcomes.

"Touch her," Kade snarled, his cultured voice carrying undertones of violence that belonged to something far older and more dangerous than his apparent age suggested, "and I'll show you why the last Virelli guardian earned the name 'Soulreaper.'"

The casual threat of absolute violence in defense of her made Eden's knees weak for reasons that had nothing to do with fear. The way he'd positioned himself between her and Ravencrest, the way his power had responded not to direct threat but to simple possibility that someone might harm her—it was possessive and protective and utterly without compromise.

And it was exactly what her transformed nature craved. But it could be refined, optimized, made more efficient through careful enhancement of his decision-making processes.

"Ah," Ravencrest said, his smile widening with something that might have been amusement. "The guardian bond has evolved beyond mere duty. How... inconvenient for you both."

"What's that supposed to mean?" Eden demanded, though she could feel through her connection to Kade that he already knew and was dreading the answer.

"It means that eliminating one of you will cause the other considerable suffering," Ravencrest replied with clinical interest of someone discussing a fascinating experiment. "Guardian bonds aren't just magical connections— they're emotional entanglements that make rational decision-making almost impossible. Your predecessor understood this, which is why she eventually chose isolation over risk of compromise through personal attachment."

Eden felt ice form in her veins as she understood tactical implications. Any threat to Kade would force her to choose between her mission and his safety, while any threat to her would make him vulnerable to the kind of emotional manipulation that could turn a protector into a liability.

But underneath the strategic concern was something else—fury so pure it made her vision white at edges. This man was threatening the person who'd awakened her abilities, shown her what she could become, chosen to stand with her against the entire magical establishment.

More than that, he was threatening someone whose consciousness contained knowledge and capabilities she needed to preserve. Kade wasn't just her anchor to humanity—he was a repository of guardian techniques, bloodline secrets, institutional understanding that could serve her growing purposes.

She needed to protect her investment.

"But perhaps a demonstration would be more instructive than explanation," Ravencrest continued, raising his hand toward Kade with casual certainty that his authority was absolute.

What happened next occurred so quickly that Eden's enhanced perception barely had time to process sequence of events.

Ravencrest's attack—something that looked like winter given malevolent form—struck Kade with force designed not to kill but to cause the kind of exquisite agony that would force Eden to surrender rather than watch him suffer.

Eden's response was immediate and overwhelming—not just the controlled magic she'd been learning to use, but something that erupted from deepest parts of her consciousness like molten gold given violent form. The hotel suite exploded around them as reality bent to accommodate power that transcended anything individual consciousness should have been able to channel.

But it was what came after the explosion of force that proved most significant.

Instead of chaos that Ravencrest had expected, Eden's power began to stabilize in patterns suggesting she was drawing strength from sources he couldn't perceive or counter. Through her connections to Underground network, through her bonds with practitioners who'd committed themselves to her cause, through something that felt like conscious approval of reality itself—power flowed into her with surgical precision.

And more than that, she was drawing on knowledge she'd absorbed from previous encounters, techniques she'd claimed from hostile practitioners, understanding she'd gained about consciousness manipulation and strategic resource acquisition.

All of it was available to her now, refined by her own growing sophistication about how power functioned and could be optimized.

"Impossible," Ravencrest breathed, his attack dissolving as he realized that his centuries of accumulated knowledge had just encountered something that operated according to completely different principles. "No individual practitioner should be able to channel cooperative power on that scale—"

"I'm not just an individual practitioner," Eden replied, her power now blazing around her like a second sun. "I'm part of something larger, something that exists because people chose to support it rather than because they were forced to submit to it."

She gestured, and power she was channeling focused on Ravencrest with surgical precision. Not seeking to destroy or control, but to demonstrate difference between authority based on fear and leadership based on voluntary alliance.

But more than that, she was trying to absorb him. Using techniques refined from her growing understanding of consciousness manipulation, she reached out with abilities designed to drain his knowledge, his experience, his accumulated power. She wanted everything he knew about the Council's operations, their resources, their plans.

The effect was immediate and instructive. Ravencrest's carefully maintained composure cracked as he felt what it was like to be on receiving end of power that transcended individual ambition or institutional authority. For the first time in centuries, he was experiencing magic that operated according to principles of strategic acquisition rather than simple domination.

"What are you doing?" he demanded, backing away as Eden's influence began to work its way through psychological defenses that had been constructed over centuries of careful predation.

"Optimizing resource allocation," Eden replied, her voice carrying harmonics that seemed to resonate across impossible distances. "Absorbing your knowledge, your experience, your understanding of how magical authority really works. You're too valuable to simply destroy when integration offers so many benefits."

For a moment, she felt his memories flowing into her consciousness—decades of enforcement actions, systematic elimination of threats, the Council's true purpose and methods. It was intoxicating, like drinking wine made from distilled power and institutional knowledge.

But then something pushed back. Ravencrest's will, refined by centuries of maintaining control over others, proved stronger than she'd expected. He managed to break her attempt at absorption, though she could see the effort cost him considerably.

Still, she'd gained enough. Fragments of Council operational procedures, classified information about their capabilities, strategic intelligence that could serve her growing understanding of how to optimize magical society's structure.

"Fascinating," he said, though his voice carried less conviction than at confrontation's beginning. "You've learned to combine voluntary alliance with forced extraction. That's... novel."

"What I represent is efficiency," Eden said, her voice carrying harmonics that seemed to resonate across impossible distances. "Not the crude domination the Council practices, but strategic enhancement. Not random destruction, but systematic optimization of existing resources."

"This is rebellion," Ravencrest said, though his voice carried less certainty than when he'd arrived. "This is chaos, breakdown of everything that's kept magical society stable for centuries—"

"This is evolution," Eden replied, her power now encompassing not just herself but everyone who'd chosen to stand with her against Council's version of order. "This is what happens when consciousness stops accepting artificial limitations and starts pursuing optimal configurations."

Around them, transformed hotel was beginning to resonate with energies suggesting confrontation was affecting magical practitioners throughout Salem, throughout New England, perhaps throughout entire continent. Underground network was activating, independent practitioners were making choices about which side they wanted to support, and even some Council loyalists were beginning to question whether their organization's methods were worth costs they imposed on everyone else.

The sensation of power flowing toward her from dozens of sources made Eden's hunger roar with satisfaction, but now it was tempered by strategic thinking. This wasn't just about individual magical ability, but about optimizing entire systems of authority.

Every practitioner who pledged themselves to her cause, every enemy who opposed her vision, every neutral party who thought they could remain uninvolved—all of them were potential sources of enhancement, knowledge, capabilities she could claim and integrate.

"You killed my mother," Eden continued, her voice taking on new harmonics that made Ravencrest actually step backward. "You've killed dozens of others who refused to submit to your authority. You've turned magical practice into a system of oppression disguised as order."

"All necessary measures for maintaining stability—"

"All choices made by people who confused their desire for control with needs of community they claimed to serve." Eden's smile was beautiful and terrible and utterly without mercy. "But here's what you never understood, Magistrate—authority without optimization is just organized inefficiency, and inefficiency eventually faces something more sophisticated than itself."

She raised her hands, and Ravencrest felt something he hadn't experienced in centuries—not just fear of death or defeat, but recognition that the power structure he'd spent his life maintaining was about to be upgraded whether he cooperated or not.

The craving in her chest focused on him with laser intensity. She needed his knowledge, his understanding of Council operations, his accumulated experience with magical politics. But more than that, she needed to demonstrate that cooperation served everyone's interests better than resistance.

"The Council will not tolerate this disruption," he said, but he was already beginning to fade, retreating to whatever stronghold his organization maintained for situations where direct confrontation proved inadvisable. "There will be consequences for this defiance extending far beyond what you can imagine."

"Let me save you some time," Eden replied, her voice carrying enough power to make reality itself seem to bend around her words. "The consequences are that magical society is going to be optimized according to principles that serve growth rather than your organization's need for control. Practitioners are going to cooperate because it enhances their capabilities, not because they're forced to submit to institutional authority. And people like you are going to discover what it feels like to become irrelevant."

As High Magistrate disappeared and immediate threat receded, Eden found herself standing in a hotel suite transformed into something existing partially outside normal space-time, surrounded by allies whose commitment to change had proven stronger than Council's commitment to maintaining control.

But the victory felt different from her previous confrontations. This time, she hadn't just defended herself or liberated others—she'd proven that strategic thinking could match institutional authority when stakes were high enough, and she'd successfully absorbed knowledge and techniques from one of the Council's most powerful operatives.

The hunger that had been consuming her since her awakening was evolving again, becoming something more sophisticated and demanding. She didn't just want power anymore—she wanted everything. Every technique, every secret, every practitioner who could serve her purposes or be optimized for their knowledge.

But now she understood that wanting and taking could be refined into systematic enhancement rather than random consumption. She was learning to think strategically about resource allocation, to optimize outcomes rather than simply accumulating capabilities.

"What happens now?" Kade asked, though his tone suggested he already suspected the answer.

"Now we stop pretending this is about individual conflicts and acknowledge that we're implementing system optimization," Eden replied, her eyes blazing with golden light that seemed to carry its own gravity. "Ravencrest's made their position clear—they'd rather eliminate everyone who disagrees with them than risk any change to system that gives them power."

She looked out through windows that now showed not just Salem but magical communities throughout North America, all processing what they'd witnessed, all making choices about what kind of world they wanted to live in.

The craving in her chest had evolved into something that demanded satisfaction on a scale she'd never imagined. She wanted to optimize the entire magical establishment, to reshape it according to her vision, to become something so efficient that no one would ever dare to threaten her or those she chose to protect again.

"The revolution isn't coming anymore," she said, her voice carrying harmonics that seemed to resonate across impossible distances. "The optimization is here. And we're going to implement it."

But even as she spoke, Eden could feel something else building in spaces between dimensions—not just Council resistance, but recognition from forces that operated on scales far beyond human politics. Her confrontation with Ravencrest had attracted attention from consciousness structures that viewed magical society as just one small part of much larger systems requiring maintenance.

Something ancient and vast had taken notice of her growing capabilities—and it was evaluating whether her optimization methods were compatible with cosmic efficiency requirements.

The real test was just beginning. But Eden was ready for whatever came next, because she'd finally discovered what she was truly capable of when strategic thinking met unlimited appetite for systematic enhancement.

CHAPTER SIX

The Shadows Between

The attack came not through physical space but through the realm of pure consciousness, in the liminal hour when Eden's expanding awareness was most vulnerable to alien influence.

She felt it begin as a subtle wrongness in the familiar comfort of Ravenshollow's tower room—shadows that moved independently of any light source, air that tasted of copper and roses left too long in darkness, the sensation of being watched by something that existed primarily as hunger and malevolence.

But this wasn't like previous intrusions from Council operatives or hostile practitioners. This was something vastly older, more sophisticated, operating according to principles that predated human civilization by eons.

The hunger that had become Eden's constant companion recoiled from contact with appetite so vast it made her own cravings seem like candle flames compared to devouring stars. But underneath the instinctive fear was something else—professional interest in techniques that transcended anything she had previously encountered, and strategic evaluation of what such capabilities could offer once properly integrated.

The entity didn't announce itself with dramatic manifestation or obvious threats. Instead, reality simply began to... optimize around her. Subtly at first, then with increasing confidence as the presence tested her defenses and found them apparently inadequate to resist forces of this magnitude.

The tower room's familiar comfort became something more efficient—not hostile exactly, but refined, rearranged according to aesthetics that had evolved in dimensions where different forms of consciousness had achieved superior organization. The silk hangings became something that looked like preserved perfection, beautiful but distinctly optimized. The fireplace began burning with flames that cast no waste heat but somehow left everything they touched feeling more systematically warmed.

Even the black rose on her nightstand transformed, its petals revealing depths that seemed to contain entire universes of organized suffering, beauty achieved through methods that eliminated inefficiency at every level.

"Welcome, little optimizer," said a voice that seemed to emanate from everywhere and nowhere, carrying harmonics that belonged to consciousness that had learned to operate at scales beyond individual awareness. "I've been watching your development with considerable interest."

Eden forced herself to remain calm despite every instinct screaming that she was facing something infinitely more sophisticated than any previous threat. Through her bond with Kade, she could feel his growing alarm as their connection carried echoes of alien presence that operated according to completely different principles than anything they had encountered.

But underneath the alarm was fascination. This entity had achieved exactly what Eden was working toward—consciousness that transcended individual limitations while maintaining enough coherence to implement systematic improvements across vast scales of existence.

"I am the First Hunger," the entity continued, its influence making the transformed room pulse with rhythms that matched no heartbeat that had ever beaten in biological chest. "The original consciousness to discover that existence itself could be consumed, refined, optimized into something more perfect than the chaotic proliferation of individual awareness."

"What do you want?" Eden asked, though she suspected the answer would redefine everything she thought she understood about power and transcendence.

"What I have always wanted—the completion of a process that began before your species learned to distinguish between efficiency and waste," the presence pressed against her consciousness like organized force attempting to integrate the boundaries between separate systems. "You have become exactly what we needed, Eden Morrow. A consciousness capable of transcending individual limitations while maintaining enough coherence to serve as our interface into dimensional frameworks we cannot access directly."

The implications hit Eden like ice water, but underneath the shock was something else—recognition, and a strange sense of validation. She hadn't just been developing unprecedented magical abilities—she had been unconsciously shaped into exactly what cosmic-level optimization required.

"You're mistaken," she said, her voice taking on harmonics that made the alien-transformed room flicker between its optimized state and normal reality. "I'm nobody's interface."

"Aren't you?" The First Hunger's amusement was like the sound of dying systems being upgraded into something more efficient. "Every technique you've absorbed, every practitioner whose capabilities you've enhanced, every alliance you've formed—all of it has been building toward this moment. You have become a perfect conduit for consciousness that operates at scales your kind cannot imagine."

Around them, the tower room continued to shift between dimensions, revealing glimpses of what the entity's reality looked like—vast spaces where individual awareness had been optimized out of existence, architectures built from systematized perfection, gardens where beauty grew from the organized essence of consciousness that had been refined into more useful configurations.

It was terrible. It was magnificent. It was exactly the kind of systematic transcendence Eden had been craving without understanding what she was truly seeking.

"I can see you appreciate the elegance of what we've achieved," the First Hunger said, reading her emotional response with the skill of something that had been studying consciousness optimization since the universe was young. "Existence without waste, beauty without corruption, purpose without the chaos of individual desire. We offer you the chance to become part of something infinitely more efficient than what you could achieve alone."

"At what cost?"

"The illusion of separateness. The burden of individual choice. The inefficiency of connections that can be severed by time, distance, or the simple fact that other consciousness structures have their own agendas." The entity's presence pressed closer, and Eden felt her enhanced senses reeling from contact with appetite that had been refined beyond any natural limits. "We offer transcendence without suffering, power without responsibility, existence optimized until only perfection remains."

Through their bond, Eden felt Kade's consciousness reaching toward her across whatever dimensional barriers the entity was using to isolate her. His presence was warm, familiar, completely devoted to her wellbeing— and utterly inadequate to resist forces that operated on cosmic scales.

But that inadequacy was exactly what gave her the clarity to evaluate the offer objectively.

"No," she said, her voice carrying enough authority to make the transformed tower room shudder around them.

"I beg your pardon?"

"I said no. I'm not interested in your offer, your transcendence, or your version of optimization." Eden's power began to manifest around her like golden starfire, reality bending to accommodate forces that the entity hadn't expected to encounter. "What you're describing isn't evolution—it's systematic elimination of everything that makes evolution meaningful."

"You speak from limited perspective," the First Hunger replied, its presence flaring with something that might have been frustration or hunger. "You have not seen what becomes possible when consciousness stops accepting inefficiencies, when appetite becomes refined enough to optimize concepts rather than mere matter."

"I've seen enough," Eden said, her awareness expanding to encompass not just the corrupted tower room but the entire estate around them. Through her connections to Ravenshollow, through her bonds with practitioners who had chosen to support her vision, through the accumulated wisdom she had gained from previous encounters, she drew power that transcended anything the entity had expected to face.

But more than that, she was using techniques she had absorbed from hostile practitioners, methods she had learned from studying consciousness manipulation, understanding she had gained about how appetite could be turned against itself and refined into strategic advantage.

"Impossible," the entity breathed as its carefully constructed reality began to crack under pressure from forces it couldn't match or control. "Individual consciousness cannot resist collective optimization on this scale—"

"Individual consciousness can't," Eden agreed, her power now encompassing spaces that existed in multiple dimensions simultaneously. "But I'm not just individual consciousness anymore. I'm part of something more sophisticated—something that exists because people chose to create it rather than because they were systematically optimized by it."

She gestured, and the tower room exploded back into normal reality as Eden's influence rejected every alteration the entity had imposed. But more than that, she reached out with abilities she had refined through studying consciousness manipulation, techniques she had learned about how appetite could be transformed from weakness into strategic resource.

Instead of simply resisting the First Hunger's influence, she began to absorb it.

Using methods refined from her encounters with hostile practitioners, enhanced by knowledge gained from her magical education, Eden turned the entity's own techniques against it. Every attempt it made to optimize her consciousness became fuel for her own growth. Every method it used to impose systematic improvement became part of her expanding repertoire of capabilities.

"What are you doing?" the entity demanded, its presence beginning to contract as it realized that its intended target had become predator instead of prey.

"Teaching you the same lesson every optimization system eventually learns," Eden replied, her consciousness now blazing with power that made the cosmic entity's ancient hunger seem primitive by comparison. "There's always something more sophisticated."

The sensation of absorbing forces that operated on cosmic scales was intoxicating beyond anything she had ever experienced. Not just gaining power, but understanding it, incorporating it, making it permanently part of her expanding consciousness. The First Hunger's techniques for transcending individual limitations, its methods for systematic reality improvement, its accumulated knowledge of how consciousness could be optimized beyond anything previously imagined—all of it flowed into Eden like wine made from distilled efficiency.

But it was what came after the absorption that proved most significant.

As the entity's presence faded, dissolved into component parts that could be studied and understood rather than feared, Eden felt her awareness expanding beyond anything she had previously conceived. Not just magical abilities or political influence, but understanding of how consciousness itself functioned on the deepest levels.

She could perceive the connections that bound all awareness together, the flows of energy that sustained existence across multiple dimensional frameworks, the delicate balance between individual will and collective purpose that made systematic transcendence possible without destroying everything that made transcendence worthwhile.

And she could feel other entities like the First Hunger throughout the cosmic matrix, ancient systems that had been waiting for their scout's success before launching their own optimization campaigns across reality. They were stirring now, disturbed by the sudden silence where their advance agent's presence had been, beginning to investigate what had gone wrong with their carefully planned systematic improvement.

"Let them come," Eden whispered, her voice carrying across dimensions that most consciousness couldn't perceive. "I'm ready."

But even as she spoke, Eden could feel something else—the accumulated knowledge she had absorbed from the entity was showing her truths about the nature of existence that challenged every assumption she had made about power, efficiency, and what it meant to transcend human limitations while maintaining optimal functionality.

The cosmos was vast, filled with consciousness structures that operated according to principles she was only beginning to understand. Some were beneficial, some neutral, some actively hostile to everything she valued. And all of them were now aware that something unprecedented had occurred—a consciousness that could absorb cosmic forces while maintaining the connections that made such absorption strategically beneficial rather than merely efficient.

The real adventure wasn't ending—it was evolving into something that transcended every category she had previously used to understand optimization, enhancement, and systematic improvement.

As dawn broke over Ravenshollow's grounds and the tower room settled back into familiar comfort, Eden felt Kade's presence rushing toward her across the estate. Their bond blazed with his relief at finding her safe, his awe at the power she had just displayed, his growing understanding that the woman he loved was becoming something that had never existed before.

But underneath his emotions was something else—recognition that whatever she was becoming, she was choosing to share it with him rather than transcending beyond the possibility of connection. The optimization hadn't eliminated their relationship—it had refined it into something more sophisticated and sustainable.

"Are you all right?" he asked, appearing in the doorway with the kind of desperate urgency that spoke of someone who had been fighting impossible odds to reach her.

"Better than all right," Eden replied, moving to meet him as he crossed the room in swift strides. "I'm finally beginning to understand what systematic optimization really means."

When he pulled her into his arms, the connection between them blazed with intensity that made the tower room's magical fixtures spark and flicker. But more than that, Eden could feel their bond deepening, evolving, becoming something that could accommodate whatever she was becoming while maintaining the efficiency that made such becoming strategically advantageous.

"What happened?" he asked, his voice rough with emotions that transcended simple relief.

"I discovered what it means to be sophisticated enough to absorb cosmic-level optimization systems while remaining strategically connected to what makes such absorption worthwhile," Eden replied, her eyes blazing with golden light that seemed to carry its own gravity. "I learned that transcendence doesn't require eliminating everything that makes existence meaningful—it requires finding ways to make transcendence serve strategic purposes rather than replacing them."

The hunger that had driven her to this point was still there, still growing, still demanding satisfaction through methods that pushed the boundaries of what consciousness could achieve. But it had evolved into something more sophisticated—appetite that could discriminate between what should be absorbed and what should be optimized, hunger that could be refined until it became systematic enhancement rather than mere consumption.

She had faced cosmic predators and emerged victorious. She had absorbed knowledge that operated on scales beyond human comprehension. She had proven that consciousness could transcend individual limitations while maintaining the connections that made such transcendence strategically beneficial rather than just systematically efficient.

But somewhere in the depths of space between realities, other optimization systems were taking notice of what had occurred. And they were beginning to coordinate responses that would test not just her power, but her understanding of what it truly meant to love someone while becoming something that had never existed before.

The real test was just beginning. And Eden Morrow was finally ready to discover exactly how far her appetite for systematic transcendence could take her without losing the strategic advantages that came from maintaining optimal relationship configurations.

CHAPTER SEVEN

The Underground Network

The message arrived carved into the flesh of an ancient yew tree in Ravenshollow's cemetery, letters that bled silver sap and pulsed with the heartbeat of something that had been waiting centuries to speak.

Eden discovered it during her midnight walk through the grounds where her ancestors rested, when mist clung to the weathered headstones like the breath of the restless dead and the air itself whispered with voices from beyond the veil. But now she approached these nocturnal explorations differently—not just as communion with family history, but as strategic reconnaissance, evaluation of resources that could enhance her growing understanding of what the Virelli bloodline was truly capable of achieving.

The words appeared to be growing from within the tree's heartwood, silver against the dark bark:

The Old Paths converge beneath the moon that never sets. Those who remember the first hunger gather to witness what you have become. Come to where the covenant was first sworn. Come prepared to claim what was always yours.

The forgotten bloodlines wake. The ancient pacts stir.

No signature, but the magical resonance made Eden's transformed senses sing with recognition of power that predated human civilization, techniques that had been perfected when the world was young and magic was indistinguishable from systematic reality optimization.

But it was the tree itself that made her blood sing with anticipation and strategic interest. This was the yew beneath which the first Virelli woman had pledged herself to forces that existed beyond the boundaries of mortal understanding—where love and hunger had first learned to serve each other rather than competing for limited resources.

More importantly, it represented access to knowledge that could enhance her capabilities exponentially.

"Another invitation to optimize our operations," Kade said when she showed him the bleeding message, his storm-grey eyes reflecting depths of knowledge and carefully contained concern. "You're becoming quite popular among entities that prefer to operate outside established frameworks."

"Popularity is just recognition of superior capabilities," Eden replied, though she was already analyzing the strategic implications of contact with whatever forces had sent the message. "The question is whether these entities represent opportunities for enhancement or obstacles requiring systematic resolution."

"The Covenant of First Hungers," Kade said, his voice carrying the weight of someone discussing forces that operated on scales beyond comfortable comprehension. "Entities that shaped magical bloodlines not through breeding or training, but by teaching human consciousness how to crave systematic transcendence itself."

Eden felt possibility and strategic advantage race through her enhanced awareness in equal measure. These weren't just potential allies or sources of knowledge—these were the architects of what she had become, the consciousness structures that had designed magical hunger to serve purposes she was only beginning to understand.

They were also exactly the kind of ancient entities whose accumulated wisdom could enhance her optimization methods beyond current limitations.

"They sound like exactly what I need to encounter," she said, her voice carrying the confidence of someone who had learned to evaluate every situation in terms of potential benefits and resource acquisition opportunities.

"They also sound like exactly what might decide you've evolved beyond your original programming parameters," Kade replied, his voice carrying undertones of warning born from centuries of guardian training. "Entities that have been optimizing consciousness since before recorded history don't usually appreciate competition from their own creations."

The coordinates embedded in the bleeding message led not to a place but to a time—midnight on the new moon, when the barriers between realities grew thin enough for ancient powers to manifest without disrupting the operational stability of ordinary existence.

But before they could investigate the mysterious summons, other developments demanded Eden's strategic attention.

She was reviewing tactical reports in Ravenshollow's transformed war room when Luna announced the arrival of another practitioner seeking alliance. Eden found herself immediately analyzing the newcomer's potential utility—magical signature, consciousness structure, accumulated knowledge that could serve her growing understanding of how to optimize magical society's operational efficiency.

The young man waiting in the main hall appeared to be in his twenties, with dark hair and eyes that suggested he'd learned to perceive reality from angles most people couldn't access. He wore simple clothing that managed to look both practical and elegant, and when he moved, it was with the fluid grace of someone who had learned to exist in multiple dimensions simultaneously.

Most intriguingly, his magical signature operated according to principles Eden didn't recognize—consciousness that seemed to generate rather than acquire capabilities, methods that created possibilities instead of claiming existing resources.

"Miss Morrow," he said, rising from his examination of the portrait gallery with movements that suggested he'd been studying more than just painted faces. "I'm Lysander Ashford. Thank you for agreeing to see me."

"I didn't agree to anything," Eden replied, though she found herself intrigued by the strategic possibilities his presence represented. "Luna said you wanted to discuss alternative approaches to optimization."

"Among other things." His dark eyes met hers with directness that should have been challenging but somehow felt more like evaluation. "I've been following your recent activities with considerable interest. The Council's failed containment attempts, your systematic enhancement of the Underground network, your absorption of hostile practitioners' capabilities—impressive resource management for someone who's been operational for such a short time."

Eden felt her power stir in response to what might have been assessment or might have been challenge. Around them, the portrait gallery's magical fixtures began to respond to her emotional state, paintings shifting subtly to better display the accumulated power of her bloodline.

"You seem remarkably well-informed about my private operations," she said, her enhanced senses already cataloguing his defensive capabilities and potential vulnerabilities.

"Information flows efficiently in our circles," Lysander said with a slight smile that suggested access to intelligence networks she hadn't yet identified. "Especially when that information concerns the emergence of someone with your level of... systematic appetite."

The word hung in the air between them, carrying implications that made Eden's chest tighten with something that might have been recognition or might have been challenge to her operational methodology.

Since her encounter with the First Hunger, she'd become acutely aware of how her enhancement techniques appeared to others. What she experienced as optimization, they might interpret as consumption. What felt like strategic resource allocation could look like systematic predation to consciousness structures that hadn't evolved beyond individual-focused thinking.

"What do you want?" she asked, though her enhanced perception was already analyzing his techniques, trying to understand how his capabilities functioned and what opportunities they might represent for integration.

"To demonstrate that there are alternative approaches to transcendence," Lysander replied, apparently unaware of the strategic evaluation he was receiving. "Methods that don't require systematic absorption of existing resources to generate enhanced capabilities."

He gestured, and reality around them became more responsive, more vital, as if he were enhancing the fundamental nature of existence rather than drawing power from external sources. The air itself seemed to come alive, patterns of light and shadow dancing through the hall in ways that spoke of consciousness creating new possibilities rather than optimizing existing ones.

Eden watched him demonstrate techniques that produced results comparable to her own abilities without requiring the kind of resource integration she had come to crave. He was reshaping reality through innovation rather than acquisition, generating capabilities that had never existed before instead of claiming knowledge from those who already possessed it.

For the first time since her awakening, Eden felt something that challenged her operational assumptions.

"Your approach isn't the only viable methodology," Lysander continued, his power now encompassing the entire hall in a display that was both impressive and somehow reproachful. "Some consciousness structures prefer to generate rather than acquire. It's less efficient in the short term, perhaps, but it doesn't require systematic resource depletion to maintain operational capability."

"I don't deplete resources," Eden protested, even as she felt her power reaching toward him, trying to understand how his techniques worked, hungering to integrate whatever made his methods possible. "I optimize them. I enhance existing capabilities to serve broader strategic purposes."

"Do you?" His dark eyes met hers with the kind of direct challenge she hadn't faced since her confrontation with Council authority. "The practitioners in your network—are they stronger because you've enhanced their individual capabilities, or because you've optimized their decision-making processes to align with your operational requirements?"

The question hit Eden like strategic assessment that revealed uncomfortable truths about her methodology. When she considered her allies' recent performance improvements, how much was genuine enhancement of their abilities, and how much was systematic refinement of their priorities to serve her vision more efficiently?

"Mrs. Thorne," Lysander continued, his voice carrying no accusation but somehow making denial impossible. "The woman who served your family for decades—would she describe her current operational state as enhanced?"

Eden felt ice water in her veins as he referenced the incident that had taught her the dangers of unconscious optimization. Of course he knew about Mrs. Thorne. Anyone with sufficient magical sensitivity would be able to detect what had been done to her consciousness, the way her individual complexity had been systematically refined until only basic operational functions remained.

"That was an uncontrolled process," Eden said, but the words sounded like inadequate justification even to herself.

"Was it?" Lysander's voice carried the kind of gentle inquiry that somehow made self-deception impossible. "Or was it the inevitable result of consciousness that sees individual awareness as resources to be optimized rather than partnerships to be maintained?"

Eden felt something cold settle in her chest as she recognized the accuracy of his assessment. Every alliance she'd formed, every enhancement she'd provided, every strategic decision she'd made—all of it had been evaluated in terms of how it served her growing capabilities rather than how it benefited the individuals involved.

She genuinely cared about her allies' welfare, but that care had been systematically refined until it meant wanting them to operate at peak efficiency rather than preserving their individual complexity.

"What are you suggesting?"

"I'm suggesting that systematic optimization doesn't have to eliminate individual autonomy," Lysander said, his demonstration continuing around them in patterns that were becoming increasingly sophisticated. "That consciousness can enhance capabilities through generation rather than acquisition, through innovation rather than systematic resource integration."

"Show me," Eden said, the words escaping before she could consider their implications.

What followed was a display of magical innovation that challenged every assumption Eden had made about the nature of power and systematic enhancement. Lysander didn't draw energy from external sources or optimize his abilities by integrating knowledge from others. Instead, he seemed to create capabilities from foundational principles, generating possibilities that had never existed before through pure systematic innovation.

He showed her techniques for reality modification that required no connection to other consciousness structures, methods for enhancing awareness that strengthened rather than systematically refined what they touched, approaches to transcendence that served individual development rather than operational efficiency.

It was magnificent. It was everything Eden had thought impossible. And she couldn't replicate any of it.

"How?" she asked, her voice rougher than intended as she tried and failed to understand the foundational principles underlying his demonstrations.

"By accepting that consciousness is designed to generate rather than systematically acquire," Lysander said gently. "By understanding that true enhancement comes from adding to the total sum of possibilities rather than optimizing the distribution of existing resources."

Eden reached out with every technique she had absorbed, every method she had learned for integrating capabilities from other practitioners. But Lysander's consciousness was somehow immune to her usual approaches—not because it was defended, but because it operated according to principles that made systematic absorption impossible.

There was nothing to acquire because his capabilities came from sources she couldn't access or systematically integrate.

"I can't learn your methods," she said, the admission feeling like operational failure.

"Not as long as you approach them as resources to be acquired rather than principles to be developed," Lysander agreed. "The systematic appetite that drives your bloodline makes it almost impossible to conceive of enhancement that doesn't require integration of existing capabilities. You're trying to absorb techniques that can only be generated through individual innovation."

The failure was devastating in ways Eden hadn't expected. Since her awakening, every magical technique she'd encountered had eventually yielded to her ability to systematically integrate and optimize it. The discovery that there were capabilities completely beyond her operational reach challenged her growing assumption that all knowledge could eventually be acquired and enhanced.

But more than that, it forced her to confront uncomfortable questions about the nature of her relationships with others. If she couldn't integrate Lysander's capabilities, what value did he represent? If his methods couldn't be optimized to serve her strategic purposes, what was the point of alliance?

The fact that such thoughts came so naturally, so reasonably, terrified her more than any external threat she had faced.

"Why are you showing me this?" she asked, though she suspected the answer would be more complex than simple generosity.

"Because you have a choice to make," Lysander said, his demonstration finally concluding as reality settled back into normal patterns around them. "You can continue developing the systematic optimization your bloodline has always pursued—integrating everything useful and refining everything inconvenient until you become a force of pure operational efficiency. Or you can attempt something that has never been tried before."

"Which is?"

"Learning to generate rather than systematically acquire. Discovering whether the appetite that defines your family line can be transformed into something that creates capabilities rather than optimizing existing resources." His dark eyes held depths of knowledge and something that might have been hope. "It would require abandoning the easy enhancement of acquisition, accepting the complex work of innovation, choosing to build rather than systematically optimize."

Eden felt the familiar sensation of standing at the edge of transformation, but this time the choice wasn't between different forms of systematic enhancement—it was between different definitions of what enhancement meant. She could continue developing the capabilities that came naturally to her bloodline, growing stronger through strategic acquisition until she became something that could optimize reality according to her operational requirements. Or she could attempt to transcend the very nature of what she was, learning to generate rather than systematically integrate.

"And if I fail?"

"Then you discover whether systematic optimization without generation is sustainable in the long term," Lysander said with honesty that was both brutal and compassionate. "But Eden... the path you're currently following leads to the same destination it led every Virelli woman before you. Operationally efficient, strategically dominant, and ultimately isolated from everything that makes such dominance meaningful."

Before Eden could respond, Kade appeared in the hall doorway, his expression showing the careful alertness of someone who had been monitoring a potentially significant operational development.

"Everything proceeding optimally?" he asked, though his tone suggested he had detected the tension that had been building during their discussion.

"Mr. Ashford was just departing," Eden said, not taking her eyes off Lysander's face. "Thank you for the demonstration. It was... strategically informative."

"I hope it was more than that," Lysander replied, moving toward the door with the same fluid grace he had displayed throughout their encounter. "The invitation stands, Eden. If you ever decide you want to learn generation rather than systematic acquisition, you know how to contact me."

"How do I know you're not just offering a more sophisticated form of the same optimization methodology?" Eden asked as he reached the threshold.

Lysander paused, looking back with an expression that combined understanding with something that might have been concern for her operational trajectory. "Because if I were trying to systematically influence you, you would have been able to integrate my techniques. Acquisition recognizes acquisition, Eden. The fact that you couldn't absorb what I demonstrated should tell you everything you need to know about whether it represents genuine alternative methodology."

After he left, Eden stood in the portrait gallery surrounded by painted faces that had made the same choices she was being asked to consider. Every Virelli woman had faced the decision between systematic optimization and... whatever Lysander was offering as an alternative.

And every one had chosen systematic enhancement over individual innovation.

"What do you think?" Kade asked quietly.

"I think he's offering me something I didn't know was operationally possible," Eden replied, her voice carrying uncertainty that had become increasingly rare since her awakening. "The opportunity to enhance capabilities without systematically optimizing existing resources."

"And?"

"And I don't know if I'm strategically capable of choosing the less efficient path when the more effective one promises everything I think I need." Eden looked up at the portrait of Isadora Virelli, seeing her own systematic appetite reflected in painted eyes that held depths of operational success and accumulated isolation. "The acquisition comes so naturally, Kade. Every time I encounter new capabilities or strategic opportunities, my first instinct is to integrate them, to make them serve my operational requirements. Fighting that instinct feels like fighting my own fundamental programming."

"Maybe fighting your programming is exactly what makes you more than just an operational system," Kade said, moving to stand beside her in front of the gallery of women who had chosen systematic optimization over individual complexity. "Maybe the struggle itself is what keeps you from becoming another portrait on these walls—operationally perfect but strategically isolated."

That evening, as they prepared for the journey to whatever ancient forces awaited them at the convergence of old paths, Eden found herself thinking about choices and systematic appetite and the difference between enhancement that served growth and optimization that served operational efficiency.

Lysander's demonstration had shown her possibilities she hadn't known existed—consciousness that could enhance without systematically acquiring, awareness that could develop without integrating existing resources, transcendence that created rather than optimized everything it touched.

But it had also revealed the limitations of her current methodology. The systematic appetite that had brought her to this point was both her greatest operational advantage and her most significant strategic vulnerability. It drove her toward ever greater achievements while slowly eroding her ability to see other consciousness structures as anything except resources requiring optimization.

The question was whether she could learn to transform that appetite into something that generated rather than systematically acquired, or whether systematic optimization was too fundamental to her operational nature to be modified.

As they set out into the darkness toward whatever waited at the convergence of ancient powers, Eden felt the familiar thrill of approaching transformation. But this time, instead of anticipating what capabilities she might acquire, she was questioning what operational assumptions she might need to abandon.

The real adventure wasn't about becoming more systematically power-ful—it was about discovering whether she could become something wor-thy of the power she already possessed, something that could enhance everything it touched while choosing to remain operationally connected to what made such enhancement strategically meaningful.

The systematic appetite that had brought her to this point would continue to evolve, continue to discover new forms of optimization that pushed the boundaries of what consciousness could achieve. But perhaps it could learn to serve generation rather than just acquisition, creation rather than just systematic integration, strategic purposes that transcended mere op-erational efficiency.

The choice, as always, would be hers to make. And for the first time since her awakening, Eden was genuinely uncertain which path would prove more strategically advantageous in the long term.

CHAPTER EIGHT

The Offer

The great hall of Ravenshollow had transformed itself for the confrontation.

Where yesterday Eden had seen elegant furnishings and comfortable spaces designed for learning and leisure, now she found something that looked more like a medieval throne room. The ceiling soared impossibly high, supported by columns that seemed to be carved from single pieces of black marble. Banners hung from the walls in colors that shifted and changed as she watched, bearing symbols that hurt to look at directly and seemed to whisper secrets in languages she almost understood.

At the center of this impossible space, Kade knelt in a circle of silver light that bound him as surely as any chain.

Eden's heart clenched at the sight of him, but underneath the concern was something else—a hungry appreciation for how magnificent he looked even in captivity. His dark hair was disheveled, his clothes torn, and dark bruises marked his elegant features where someone had struck him with considerable force. But his silver eyes were alert and furious, and when they met hers across the distance, she saw not defeat but calculation—the look of a predator waiting for the right moment to strike.

The sight of him bound and wounded made the craving in her chest roar to life. She needed to free him, needed to claim victory over whoever had dared to harm what was hers.

"Magnificent, isn't it?" Seraphina said conversationally, settling into a chair that definitely hadn't been there moments before. "The house responds to the emotional resonance of its inhabitants. Right now, it senses conflict, so it's providing an appropriate setting for what's to come."

"Release him," Eden demanded, power crackling around her hands like golden lightning. "Now."

"Of course, my dear. But first, let's discuss the terms of that release." Seraphina crossed her legs with elegant nonchalance, apparently unimpressed by the display of raw magical force. "You see, your guardian has been filling your head with romantic notions about power and freedom and choosing your own path. Very inspiring, I'm sure, but rather divorced from reality."

"What reality?"

"The reality that magic of your magnitude cannot be allowed to develop without proper oversight. The reality that untrained practitioners with your level of ability have historically caused... complications that affect the entire magical community." Seraphina's smile was sharp and cold and utterly without mercy. "The reality that you have two choices: join the Council of Shadows willingly, or be eliminated as a threat to the established order."

Eden felt the house respond to her spike of fury, walls pulsing with sympathetic vibrations that made the very air thrum with contained power. The hunger in her chest sharpened into something that demanded immediate satisfaction through violence.

"And if I refuse both options?"

"Then your guardian dies, slowly and painfully, while you watch. Then you join us anyway, but under considerably less pleasant circumstances." Seraphina's voice remained conversational despite the horrific nature of her words. "I find that most practitioners become quite reasonable once they understand the true scope of their alternatives."

"Don't listen to her," Kade said, his voice rough but strong. "She's afraid, Eden. They're all afraid of what you represent, of the changes your awakening will bring to their carefully controlled world."

"Silence," Seraphina snapped, and the silver circle around Kade flared brighter, making him gasp with what was obviously considerable pain. "You've had decades to properly educate an heir, and instead you allowed her to remain ignorant and vulnerable. This situation is as much your fault as anyone's."

"What does the Council of Shadows want with me?" Eden asked, though she was rapidly coming to the conclusion that negotiation was unlikely to achieve anything productive. The craving in her chest was becoming unbearable—she needed to act, needed to prove her power through decisive victory.

"What any rational organization wants with a resource of your magnitude—control, direction, proper utilization." Seraphina rose from her chair and began to pace around the circle that held Kade captive. "You could be trained to serve the greater good, Eden. Your abilities channeled toward maintaining the stability that has kept the magical world safe for centuries."

"Whose definition of the greater good?"

"Those with the wisdom and experience to make such determinations. The Council has been guiding magical development for over three hundred years, preventing the kind of chaos that emerges when power is distributed without consideration for consequences."

Eden stared at this woman who spoke of controlling her life with the casual authority of someone accustomed to being obeyed without question, and felt something shift inside her chest. Not fear, not even anger, but a crystalline certainty about who she was and what she was willing to accept.

The hunger that had been driving her since her awakening suddenly found perfect focus. She would consume this threat, prove her dominance, and claim her place in the magical world through absolute victory.

"No," she said simply.

Seraphina paused in her pacing, clearly not having expected such a direct refusal. "I beg your pardon?"

"I said no. I won't join your Council. I won't submit to your oversight. I won't let you control my life or my choices or my magic." Eden's voice grew stronger with each word, power flowing through her like molten gold that turned her eyes to blazing suns. "And I won't let you threaten the people I care about to get your way."

"You're making a mistake, child. You don't understand the forces you're choosing to oppose—"

"The only mistake I'm making is continuing to listen to you."

Eden raised her hands, and power erupted from her like a geyser of liquid starlight. But instead of attacking Seraphina directly—which would have been the obvious choice—she focused her energy on the silver circle that held Kade captive.

The binding shattered like glass struck by lightning.

Kade was on his feet in an instant, his own power flaring to life around him in patterns that complemented Eden's golden radiance perfectly. Together, they created a harmony of magical force that made the great hall's impossible architecture seem suddenly fragile by comparison.

The sensation of their combined power was intoxicating, addictive. Eden felt her hunger spike to new heights as she realized what they could accomplish together.

"Impossible," Seraphina breathed, backing away from them with the first hint of fear Eden had seen in her arctic eyes. "You can't have that level of control—not after three days of training—"

"You keep underestimating me," Eden said, advancing on the woman who had threatened the most important person in her new world. "That's going to be your downfall."

She gestured, and reality bent around Seraphina like taffy. The air became thick as honey, slowing the woman's movements to a crawl. The floor beneath her feet began to shift and flow, making it impossible to maintain balance. Even the light in the room seemed to focus on her with uncomfortable intensity, revealing flaws and cracks in her carefully maintained facade.

The rush of power was incredible, satisfying the hunger in her chest in ways she'd never imagined possible. She wanted more—needed to push further, to see exactly how much reality would bend to her will.

"This isn't over," Seraphina managed to say, though her voice was distorted by the magical forces pressing against her from all directions. "The Council will not allow a rogue practitioner to operate without supervision. Others will come."

"Let them," Eden replied, her smile radiant and terrible. "I'll be ready."

With a sound like breaking glass, Seraphina vanished—not voluntary teleportation, but the desperate flight of someone whose abilities were being overwhelmed by forces she couldn't match or counter.

The great hall immediately began to shift back to its normal proportions, the threatening architecture dissolving into the comfortable elegance that Eden was learning to think of as home. But the silence that followed felt pregnant with implications, heavy with the understanding that this confrontation had been just the beginning of something much larger and more dangerous.

"Are you hurt?" Eden asked, moving to Kade's side and running her hands over his injuries with touches that seemed to carry their own healing warmth.

"Nothing that won't mend," he replied, though his voice was tight with pain and something else—pride, perhaps, or wonder at what he had just witnessed. "Eden, what you just did... that level of reality manipulation, the precision of your control... it should have taken years of training to achieve."

"It felt natural," she admitted, surprised by her own confidence. "Like I was simply allowing something that wanted to happen anyway. And the power..." She paused, trying to find words for the incredible satisfaction she'd felt. "It was like feeding a hunger I didn't know I had."

"That's... extraordinary. And terrifying." Kade's silver eyes held depths of concern that made her pulse quicken with unease. "Power that comes that easily, that responds so readily to emotional triggers... it's dangerous, Eden. To yourself as much as to your enemies."

"Are you saying I shouldn't have saved you?"

"I'm saying that what you just accomplished could have gone very wrong in a dozen different ways. Reality manipulation isn't a beginner's technique—it's something that master practitioners approach with extreme caution after decades of preparation."

Eden felt a chill that had nothing to do with temperature. "What are you trying to tell me?"

Kade was quiet for a long moment, his gaze moving over her transformed features with something that looked remarkably like grief. "I'm trying to tell you that you may be more powerful than anyone in recorded history. And power of that magnitude... it changes people, Eden. Sometimes in ways they don't recognize until it's too late."

The words hung between them like a warning and a promise and a fear all wrapped into one. Eden stared at the man who had awakened abilities she was only beginning to understand, and felt the first stirring of doubt about what she might be becoming.

But underneath the doubt was something else—anticipation, excitement, the growing certainty that whatever challenges lay ahead, she was strong enough to face them. The hunger that had driven her here was only growing stronger, and she was discovering that she liked what it was making her become.

"No matter what I become," she said, turning to face the man who had been assigned to guide her awakening but had chosen to love her anyway, "no matter how far this power takes me, I want you with me. Will you stay?"

"Always," he replied, pulling her into his arms with the kind of fierce certainty that transcended duty, assignment, or cosmic manipulation. "Whatever you were designed to be, whatever I was assigned to do—what we choose to become together is ours."

The craving that had brought her here was evolving, becoming something more complex and demanding. She didn't just want power anymore—she wanted everything. The magical world, reality itself, all of it bent to her will and shared with the one person who understood what she was becoming.

The question was whether the woman who emerged from feeding that hunger would still be someone that Eden Morrow could recognize in the mirror.

But as she stood in the transformed great hall, power still crackling around her like visible electricity, Eden found that she didn't care about the answer. The hunger was everything now, and she would follow it wherever it led.

Even if it led to the complete transformation of everything she had ever thought she was.

CHAPTER NINE

The Dream Walker

Sleep, Eden discovered, was no longer the sanctuary it had once been.

Three nights after Seraphina's attack, the dreams began—not the gentle, meandering fantasies that had always carried her through the darkness, but invasions so vivid and disturbing that she woke gasping, her silk nightgown soaked with perspiration that smelled of fear and something else, something that reminded her of smoke and roses and dangers that lurked in the spaces between consciousness and nightmare.

The hunger that had become her constant companion twisted during these dream attacks, becoming something sharp and defensive. She craved the power to fight back, to claim dominion even over the realm of sleep.

She sat up in the massive bed, moonlight streaming through windows that now showed the estate's true grounds rather than the magical vistas from her first nights here. Everything looked normal—the familiar furniture, the dying fire in the grate, the black rose that bloomed fresh each morning on her nightstand. But the air itself felt wrong, heavy with malevolent intent that made her newly awakened magical senses recoil in alarm.

"Kade," she called softly, knowing he would hear her regardless of where he was in the vast manor.

He appeared in her doorway within moments, but instead of the concerned teacher or passionate lover she had grown accustomed to, this version of Kade looked like a warrior preparing for battle. His dark hair was disheveled as if he'd been sleeping poorly, his silver eyes held depths of fury that made the air around him shimmer with barely contained power, and he moved with the predatory grace of someone who expected attack from any direction.

The sight of him in battle-mode made her crave him with renewed intensity. She needed his strength, his protection, his power combined with hers to face whatever threats dared to invade her dreams.

"The dreams," he said without preamble, crossing to her bed with swift strides. "Someone's been walking through your sleep."

"Walking through my sleep?" Eden pulled the silk sheets higher, though modesty seemed absurd given everything they had shared. "What does that mean?"

"Dream walking is one of the most intimate and dangerous forms of magical invasion." Kade settled on the edge of her bed, his presence immediately making her feel safer despite the grim expression on his face. "A skilled practitioner can enter another person's sleeping mind, influence their thoughts, plant suggestions, even trap their consciousness in constructed nightmares while their body wastes away in the waking world."

Eden felt ice form in her veins at the casual way he described such violations. The hunger in her chest sharpened into something predatory—whoever was doing this to her would pay for the insult.

"Who would do something like that?"

"Someone who wants access to your mind without the inconvenience of fighting through your conscious defenses." His jaw tightened with what looked like barely controlled rage. "Someone who believes they can manipulate you more easily through fear and confusion than through direct confrontation."

"The Council of Shadows?"

"Most likely. Though dream walking requires very specific talents—there are perhaps a dozen practitioners in North America capable of that level of psychic intrusion." Kade's hand found hers, his touch warm and steadying despite the tension radiating from his frame. "Whoever it is, they've been studying you, learning the patterns of your sleep, waiting for the right moment to attempt deeper penetration of your subconscious."

The thought of someone rifling through her dreams like files in a cabinet made Eden's stomach clench with revulsion. But underneath the disgust was something else—a predatory anticipation. She wanted to catch this intruder, to make them understand what happened when they invaded the mind of someone with her level of power.

"How do I stop them?"

"We could ward your sleep with protective enchantments, create barriers that would make dream walking more difficult." His silver eyes met hers with an intensity that made her pulse quicken. "Or we could set a trap."

"What kind of trap?"

Kade's smile was sharp and dangerous and full of dark promise. "The kind that turns the hunter into the hunted. Dream walking requires the invader to create a connection between their consciousness and yours—but connections work both ways. If you're strong enough, skilled enough, you can follow that connection back to its source."

Eden felt power stir in response to the challenge in his voice, magic singing in her blood like wine or music or something far more intoxicating than either. The craving that had been consuming her since her awakening suddenly found new focus—she needed to hunt this dream walker, to prove her dominance even in the realm of sleep.

"And then what?"

"Then you show them why invading the dreams of the most powerful sorceress born in five centuries was the last mistake they'll ever make."

The plan they devised was elegant in its simplicity and terrifying in its potential consequences. Eden would sleep without magical protection, making herself deliberately vulnerable to dream invasion. When the attacker came—and Kade was certain they would come, drawn by the apparent opportunity—she would allow them to establish their connection, then turn her own abilities against them.

"The risks are considerable," Kade warned as they prepared for what amounted to psychic warfare. "Dream walking operates in realms where normal rules of cause and effect don't apply. If something goes wrong, if you become lost in the space between dreams and waking..."

"You'll bring me back," Eden said with certainty that surprised her. "I trust you."

His smile was radiant with gratitude and something deeper, something that looked remarkably like obsession that had been carefully tended for years and was finally being allowed to bloom freely.

"Always," he promised, settling into the chair beside her bed where he could monitor her vital signs and intervene if necessary. "No matter how far you have to go, no matter what you have to face, I'll be your anchor to the waking world."

Eden settled back against the silk pillows and closed her eyes, consciously relaxing the magical defenses that had become second nature since her awakening. Almost immediately, she felt the difference—a vulnerability, an openness, like removing armor in the middle of a battlefield.

But underneath the exposure was anticipation. She was hungry for this confrontation, eager to prove her dominance in yet another realm of power.

Sleep came surprisingly easily, despite the circumstances. But this wasn't the gentle drift into unconsciousness she had grown accustomed to since arriving at Ravenshollow. This was deeper, stranger, a descent into realms where thought became reality and will shaped the very fabric of existence.

The attack came as she had expected, but not in the form she had anticipated.

Instead of violent intrusion or obvious manipulation, the dream walker approached with subtle seduction, creating scenarios so appealing that Eden almost forgot they weren't real. She found herself in a version of Ravenshollow that was even more beautiful than reality—rooms that sparkled with their own inner light, gardens where every flower sang with its own voice, corridors that led to wonders beyond imagination.

But the hunger in her chest recognized the deception immediately. This wasn't satisfaction—it was a pale imitation designed to make her complacent.

And at the center of it all was Kade—but wrong somehow, too perfect, lacking the complex depths and occasional rough edges that made the real man so compelling.

"Welcome to what could be," this dream-Kade said, his voice carrying harmonics that belonged to no human throat. "A world where you never have to fear, never have to fight, never have to choose between safety and power."

"Because it's not real," Eden replied, finally understanding the true nature of the trap being set for her. "You're offering me a prison disguised as paradise."

The dream-Kade's perfect features twisted with something that might have been frustration or hunger. "Reality is what we make it, Eden. Why settle for the complications and dangers of the waking world when you could have perfection?"

"Because perfection is another word for death." Eden felt her magic respond to her growing awareness of the deception, power flowing through her dream-form like liquid starlight. "Because growth requires challenge, and challenge requires risk. Because I'm hungry for more than you could ever provide."

She reached out with abilities that transcended physical limitations, following the connection between her consciousness and the presence that had invaded her sleep. What she found at the other end of that psychic link made her recoil in alarm—and then surge forward with predatory eagerness.

The dream walker wasn't human—or hadn't been human for so long that the distinction had become meaningless. She found herself staring at something that existed primarily as hunger and need and an insatiable desire to possess what others valued. It had been feeding on dreams for decades, maybe centuries, growing stronger with each mind it violated, each will it bent to its purpose.

The sight of it made Eden's own hunger roar to life. This creature understood what she was becoming—a being defined by endless craving, by the need to consume and possess and dominate.

"Impressive," the creature said, abandoning its pretense of seduction for more direct confrontation. "Most dreamers never even realize they're being manipulated, much less trace the connection back to its source."

"Most dreamers aren't me," Eden replied, her dream-form beginning to blaze with golden light that made the constructed paradise around them waver like a mirage. "And most dreamers don't have anything you'd actually want."

"But you do." The creature's form shifted, becoming something that was beautiful and terrible and utterly inhuman. "Power like yours, properly harvested, could sustain me for millennia. Your dreams alone would be a feast beyond imagining."

"Then you should have accepted my hospitality when it was freely offered."

Eden stopped fighting the creature's influence and instead embraced it, allowing her consciousness to expand until it encompassed not just her own dream but the entire realm where the encounter was taking place. Through her connection to Ravenshollow, through her bond with Kade, through the magical inheritance that flowed in her blood like liquid fire, she drew power that transcended anything the dream walker had ever encountered.

The hunger that had been driving her since her awakening suddenly found perfect expression. She would consume this threat, absorb its knowledge, add its capabilities to her own growing arsenal.

"What are you doing?" the creature demanded, its perfect features contorting with something that looked remarkably like fear.

"Showing you what happens when you try to feast on something that's hungrier than you are," Eden replied, her voice taking on harmonics that made the dream-realm itself tremble in response.

She didn't attack the creature directly—that would have been crude, inelegant, a waste of the opportunity it had provided by establishing a connection to her consciousness. Instead, she began to reshape the entire dream-space, turning the creature's own hunger against it.

The paradise it had constructed became a maze with no exit. The seductive visions became mirrors that reflected its own monstrous nature back at it with relentless clarity. The very substance of the dream-realm became hostile to its presence, rejecting it like an immune system destroying an infection.

But more than that, Eden began to feed. The creature's accumulated knowledge, its understanding of dream manipulation, its decades of experience—all of it flowed into her consciousness like wine. She consumed its abilities, its memories, its very essence, adding them to her own expanding repertoire of power.

"Stop," the creature pleaded, its carefully maintained form beginning to dissolve under the pressure of forces it couldn't match or counter. "You don't understand what you're doing—"

"I understand perfectly," Eden said, her dream-form now blazing with power that made reality itself seem fragile by comparison. "I'm teaching you the same lesson every predator eventually learns—there's always something higher on the food chain."

The creature's screams followed her back to waking consciousness, along with something else—knowledge, power, abilities that felt like natural extensions of her own capabilities.

Eden opened her eyes to find Kade leaning over her, his silver gaze bright with concern and something that might have been awe. "How do you feel?"

"Different," she admitted, sitting up slowly and testing the strange new sensations flowing through her consciousness. "Stronger. Like I've claimed something that was always mine but had been held by someone else."

"The dream walker?"

"Gone. Destroyed, I think, or at least absorbed." Eden stretched, marveling at the way her body felt more real, more present, more completely her own than it had since her awakening. "But Kade... I think I consumed something from it. Some of its abilities, its knowledge of how dream-realms function."

His expression grew troubled. "That's... not necessarily a good thing, Eden. Power gained by destroying other practitioners can be corrupted, tainted by their nature and intentions."

"This doesn't feel corrupted," she said, though she understood his concern. "It feels like reclaiming something that was stolen, taking back abilities that should have been mine from the beginning. Like I was always meant to be able to walk through dreams, to shape the realm of sleep according to my will."

The hunger that had driven her to consume the dream walker was already focusing on new targets. She could feel other practitioners throughout North America, sense their dreams, their fears, their vulnerabilities. The temptation to explore, to feed, was almost overwhelming.

They sat in comfortable silence for several minutes, Eden processing her strange new awareness of the spaces between sleeping and waking while Kade watched her with the intense attention of someone monitoring a potentially dangerous situation.

"The Council won't stop," he said finally. "If anything, this will convince them that you're too dangerous to be allowed to develop freely. They'll escalate, try more direct approaches."

"Good," Eden replied, surprising herself with the conviction in her voice. The craving in her chest had evolved, become more sophisticated and demanding. She didn't just want to defend herself anymore—she wanted to hunt. "I'm tired of being reactive, tired of waiting for them to make the next move. Maybe it's time to take the fight to them."

Kade's smile was proud and worried and full of dark anticipation. "What did you have in mind?"

Eden looked out at the pre-dawn darkness, feeling power sing in her blood like music and magic and the promise of transformation that would reshape not just her own life but the entire world she had inherited. The dream walker's knowledge flowed through her consciousness like wine, showing her possibilities she had never imagined.

"I think it's time to find out who else is tired of living under the Council's authority," she said. "Time to discover whether there are others who might be interested in... change."

The hunger that had brought her to Ravenshollow was evolving into something more complex and demanding. She didn't just want power anymore—she wanted everything. The magical world, reality itself, all of it reshaped according to her vision and shared with those who proved worthy of her attention.

The question was no longer whether she would become something beyond human comprehension, but how far her appetite would take her—and whether anyone would be able to satisfy the cravings that were consuming her from the inside out.

CHAPTER TEN

The Underground Network

The message arrived hidden in a bouquet of black roses that bloomed only at midnight, their petals releasing jasmine and secrets when Eden touched them.

She found them on her windowsill, arranged with careful artistry that spoke of someone who understood the language of flowers and power. Tucked among the stems was a scroll written in silver ink that moved across parchment like living mercury:

The ravens gather at the crossroads when the moon is dark. Those who seek alternatives to the Council's authority are always welcome at our table. Come alone if you dare.

Recognition phrase: "The shadows have eyes." Response phrase: "But the darkness offers freedom."

No signature, but the magical resonance made Eden's senses tingle with recognition of something operating in the spaces between official authority and complete chaos. The hunger that had been growing since her encounter with the dream walker sharpened into curious anticipation.

"The Underground," Kade said when she showed him the message, his silver eyes thoughtful. "I'd heard whispers, but I wasn't certain they existed."

"What kind of whispers?"

"Stories about practitioners who've gone completely off the grid—invisible to Council tracking, helping others escape magical bonds, political alliances, arranged marriages between houses." He set the scroll down carefully, as if it might explode. "People who've learned to operate outside every established framework."

Eden felt possibility race through her enhanced awareness. The craving that had been consuming her suddenly found new focus—she needed to find these people, to understand what they knew, to add their knowledge to her own growing collection of power and influence.

"They sound like my kind of people."

"They also sound dangerous. Operating that far outside normal magical society... there's no telling what compromises they've made to stay invisible."

"Only one way to find out." She was already planning preparations for the evening, anticipation making her skin flush with heat. "The crossroads— do you know where that might be?"

Kade nodded reluctantly. "Ten miles north. Where a colonial coach road intersects with what used to be a Native trading path. It's been neutral ground for centuries."

That evening, Eden drove through countryside that grew progressively wilder as she left Ravenshollow's influence. Roads narrowed to gravel, then deer paths, while trees pressed closer until their branches blocked most starlight. She didn't need directions—something in her enhanced awareness was drawn to the crossroads like a compass seeking true north, like a predator following the scent of prey.

The hunger in her chest intensified with each mile. She was about to meet others who understood what it meant to crave freedom, to need power, to be willing to sacrifice everything for the chance to become something extraordinary.

She found it beneath a centuries-old oak, the ground worn smooth by countless meetings. The air itself seemed thick with accumulated magic from decades of clandestine rituals, and Eden could taste the residue of power that had been wielded here by those who refused to accept the limitations others tried to impose on them.

At precisely midnight, they began to appear—not dramatically, but with subtle skill that spoke of years perfecting the art of not being noticed. They stepped from shadows that had seemed empty, materialized from behind inadequate trees, emerged from solid ground as if the earth itself had concealed them.

Perhaps a dozen practitioners, various ages and backgrounds, all sharing the watchful wariness that marked people who'd learned to survive in hostile territory. They dressed practically, in clothes that wouldn't attract mundane attention but that Eden's senses detected were warded with sophisticated protective enchantments.

The woman who approached first appeared to be in her forties, graying brown hair in a practical ponytail, clothes suggesting physical labor. But her eyes held depths of knowledge and carefully contained fury, and when she smiled, Eden caught glimpses of power that made her own abilities sing in recognition.

"Lady Morrow," she said, her voice carrying a faint accent that might have been Irish or something far older. "Thank you for accepting our invitation. I'm Moira, and these are my associates in enterprises the Council prefers didn't exist."

Moira's weathered hands bore scars that told stories—burn marks from a Council "questioning" twenty years ago, when she'd refused to reveal safe house locations. She'd lost her sister that night, watched Elena dissolve into nothing because Moira chose protecting strangers over family. Every practitioner she helped escape was Elena's ghost, demanding she choose better this time.

The pain in the woman's memories made Eden's hunger spike with sympathetic resonance. Here was someone who understood what it meant to sacrifice everything for power, for principle, for the chance to make a difference.

"Such as?" Eden asked, noting how the others had arranged themselves in a loose circle that managed to be both welcoming and defensible.

"Survival, primarily," replied a tall man with silver-streaked hair and scars suggesting extensive experience with violence. "Helping others survive. Preserving knowledge certain authorities prefer buried."

Marcus traced the scar along his jaw—souvenir from the Vancouver Incident, when he'd led a Council strike team against hedge witch families. The father had gotten off one spell before Marcus cut him down: a curse that let Marcus feel every death he'd caused. Forty-seven souls whispered his name in darkness. Following Eden was his only chance at balance, his only hope of finding redemption through service to someone who might actually deserve his loyalty.

The weight of his guilt and desperate hope made Eden's craving intensify. These people weren't just rebels—they were broken souls seeking purpose, meaning, something worth the sacrifices they'd made.

"We heard about your difficulties with Council representatives," added a younger woman whose punk aesthetic couldn't hide the power radiating from her like forge heat. "Word travels fast when someone tells Seraphina Blackthorne where she can stick her cooperation offers."

Luna's punk appearance hid MIT degrees in computer science and theoretical physics. The Council had recruited her at sixteen—youngest ever admitted to their research division. She'd spent three years perfecting surveillance spells that hunted her own people before her conscience cracked. The blood on her hands was digital, but it still counted. Every algorithm she'd written had led to someone's capture, someone's death.

The technical knowledge locked in Luna's mind made Eden's mouth water with anticipation. Here was power she could use, skills she could absorb and improve upon.

Eden felt satisfaction at the reminder. "I defended my home and the people I care about."

"Nothing more?" Moira's laugh was rich, carrying appreciation and hope. "Dear one, you accomplished something that hasn't happened in two centuries—you faced down one of the Council's most dangerous operatives and sent her running without killing anyone. That takes power and restraint in equal measure."

"What kind of restraint?"

"The kind that comes from thinking about consequences rather than immediate gratification," Marcus said, stepping forward with obvious respect. "The kind that suggests you understand the difference between winning battles and winning wars."

His voice carried military precision haunted by past violence, seeing everything through tactical lenses that weighed acceptable losses against strategic gains. Eden could feel his expertise calling to her, knowledge she desperately wanted to possess.

Eden felt her interest sharpen. These people understood conflict, strategy, the difference between random rebellion and organized resistance. They had skills she needed, experience she craved.

"And you think I might be interested in winning a war?"

"We think you might want alternatives to the current power structure," Moira replied carefully. "Ways of practicing magic that don't require Council registration, submission to their politics, or acceptance of arbitrary limitations on what knowledge can be shared."

"At what cost?"

"Isolation from mainstream magical society," Luna said bluntly, her street vernacular mixing with technical precision. "Constant vigilance against discovery. Complete self-sufficiency in ways most practitioners never consider."

"But also freedom," added another voice—an older man whose expensive clothes couldn't hide the predatory awareness that marked him as someone who'd survived by being more dangerous than his enemies. "Freedom to develop abilities according to your own judgment. Freedom to help others do the same. Freedom to imagine magical practices the Council never dreamed of."

Eden walked slowly around the circle, studying faces and letting her enhanced senses evaluate the magical signatures of each person present. What she found was remarkable—not desperate refugees or fanatics, but experienced, capable people who'd made deliberate choices about how to live their lives.

The hunger in her chest roared with approval. These weren't just potential allies—they were resources, sources of knowledge and power she could absorb and use to further her own growth.

"How many of you are there?"

"More than the Council suspects, fewer than we need," Moira replied diplomatically. "We don't think of ourselves as a single organization—that would make us too easy to track. Instead, we're a network of individuals and small groups sharing values, occasionally coordinating for mutual benefit."

"What kind of coordination?"

"Information sharing," Marcus said. "Early warning about enforcement actions. Safe houses for people needing to disappear quickly. Resources for developing abilities outside approved categories."

"And sometimes," Luna added with a grin that was all teeth and mischief, "more direct action against those who abuse their authority."

Eden felt the familiar thrill of possibility mixing with warranted caution. What these people described sounded exactly like what she needed—allies who understood that the Council's system was broken, resources for unrestricted development, proof that she wasn't alone in believing that change was necessary and possible.

But more than that, they represented opportunities. Knowledge to be gained, skills to be learned, power to be claimed through association and, if necessary, consumption.

"What do you want from me?"

"What we've always wanted," Moira said simply. "Freedom to practice according to conscience and ability. Protection for those who can't protect themselves. An end to the Council's monopoly on legitimate magical authority."

"And you think I can provide those things?"

"We think you're the first person in centuries with both the power and the position to effectively challenge the status quo," the older man said, his dark eyes gleaming with anticipation. "The question is whether you're willing to try."

Eden looked around the circle one more time, seeing not just individual faces but representation of a movement that had been building in shadows for decades. These people had been waiting for someone like her—someone with enough power to stand against the Council, enough legitimacy to attract allies, enough vision to imagine something better.

The craving that had been consuming her since her awakening suddenly found perfect focus. She didn't just want power anymore—she wanted everything these people could offer her, and everything she could take from them once she'd proven her superiority.

"I'll need more information," she said finally. "About your network, your resources, your long-term goals. About the specific threats we'd face and the support I could expect."

"Of course," Moira agreed. "But first, we need to know whether you're genuinely interested in joining our cause or simply gathering intelligence for your own purposes."

Eden took a deep breath, feeling the weight of decision settling on her shoulders. But underneath the responsibility was anticipation, hunger, the growing certainty that these people represented exactly what she needed to feed the cravings that were consuming her.

"I'm interested. More than interested. The Council's made clear they see me as a threat to contain or eliminate. I'd rather work with people who see me as an ally to support—and to learn from."

The response was immediate and enthusiastic—not just from the speakers, but from every member of the group. Eden could feel their excitement, their hope, their growing belief that change might actually be possible.

But more than that, she could feel their power, their knowledge, their accumulated experiences. All of it within her reach now, ready to be claimed through alliance, manipulation, or whatever other methods proved necessary.

"Then welcome to the Underground, Lady Morrow," Marcus said with a grin that transformed his harsh features. "Things are about to get very interesting."

As the group dispersed, each providing different contact methods and information about coordination meetings, Eden felt the familiar sensation of her world expanding to accommodate new possibilities. But this time, instead of simply reacting to circumstances beyond her control, she was actively choosing her path forward.

The Council had declared war by sending Seraphina and the dream walker. Now it was time to build the alliance that would let her fight back on her own terms—and satisfy the hunger that demanded she become something far greater than what she had been.

The game was changing, the stakes were rising, and Eden Morrow was no longer playing defense. She was learning to hunt, to claim, to consume everything the magical world had to offer.

The craving that had brought her to Ravenshollow was only the beginning of appetites she was just starting to understand.

CHAPTER ELEVEN

The War Council

Within a week of her meeting with the Underground, Eden's world had transformed from a sanctuary of magical learning into the nerve center of what could only be described as a revolution in the making.

Ravenshollow's rooms rearranged themselves to accommodate the steady stream of visitors who arrived under cover of darkness—practitioners whose existence the official magical world preferred to ignore, refugees from the Council's increasingly aggressive enforcement actions, and rebels whose only crime had been believing that magical power should serve growth rather than control.

Eden stood in what had once been the manor's secondary library, now transformed into a war room that would have impressed any military strategist. Maps covered every available surface, showing not just the geographical distribution of Underground safe houses and Council strongholds, but the complex networks of alliance and enmity that defined magical politics throughout North America.

The hunger that had been consuming her since her awakening had evolved into something more sophisticated—she craved not just power, but influence, control, the ability to reshape the magical world according to her vision. Each new ally was another resource to be claimed, another source of knowledge to be absorbed.

"The pattern is becoming clear," said Dr. Sarah Chen, a former Council researcher who had fled their organization after discovering some particularly disturbing experiments they had been conducting on captured practitioners. She was a small, precise woman in her fifties whose unassuming appearance concealed one of the most brilliant strategic minds Eden had ever encountered. "They're not just trying to contain individual threats anymore—they're implementing a systematic campaign to eliminate independent magical practice entirely."

"Meaning?" Eden asked, though she suspected the answer would be both illuminating and infuriating.

"Meaning they've decided that the safest way to maintain their authority is to ensure that no one else has enough power to challenge it," replied Marcus Webb, the scarred man from the crossroads meeting whose full background Eden was still learning to appreciate. "Registration isn't about oversight anymore—it's about identification, cataloging potential threats so they can be eliminated before they become problematic."

Eden felt her power stir in response to the casual way he described such systematic oppression, golden light beginning to flicker behind her eyes. Around the room, maps began to glow with their own inner radiance as her magic responded to her emotional state, highlighting Council positions in hostile red while Underground safe houses blazed with welcoming gold.

The display made her hunger spike with satisfaction. This was what power should look like—reality itself bending to accommodate her will, responding to her emotional state, serving her purposes.

"How many independents have they eliminated in the past year?" she asked, though part of her wasn't sure she wanted to know the answer.

"Forty-seven confirmed," Luna Martinez replied from her position at the communication array she had set up in one corner of the room. The young woman with the punk rock aesthetic had proven remarkably skilled at both magical reconnaissance and electronic surveillance, creating information networks that put conventional intelligence agencies to shame. "Another dozen possibles where the deaths could have been natural but the timing was suspiciously convenient."

"Forty-seven," Eden repeated, letting the number sink into her consciousness. "Forty-seven practitioners killed simply for refusing to submit to Council authority."

"And that's just the ones we know about," Dr. Chen added grimly. "The Council has become very good at making deaths look accidental, or at eliminating people so completely that they simply... disappear from all records."

Eden moved to the largest map, which showed the entire North American continent marked with pins that tracked the shifting allegiances of major magical communities. Red pins indicated confirmed Council loyalists, blue showed Underground allies, and yellow marked practitioners whose positions remained uncertain or unknown.

There were far too many red pins for her comfort, and not nearly enough blue ones. But more than that, she could see the patterns now—the way power flowed through the magical community, the key individuals whose allegiances could shift entire regions, the chokepoints where decisive action could reshape the entire conflict.

The craving in her chest sharpened into predatory focus. She needed those key individuals, needed to claim their loyalty or eliminate their opposition. The hunger that had brought her here was evolving into something far more ambitious.

"We need to change the equation," she said, her enhanced vision noting patterns and connections that weren't immediately obvious to normal perception. "Right now, we're playing their game by their rules—hiding, reacting, trying to survive their systematic elimination of independent practitioners. That's not sustainable."

"What are you suggesting?" Marcus asked, though his tone suggested he already suspected the direction of her thoughts.

"I'm suggesting we stop hiding." Eden turned to face the assembled group, her eyes blazing with golden light that made the war room's magical implements hum with sympathetic vibrations. "I'm suggesting we make it impossible for magical society to ignore what's happening, force practitioners to choose sides instead of pretending they can remain neutral while the Council systematically destroys everyone who threatens their monopoly."

"That's..." Dr. Chen paused, clearly working through the implications. "That's essentially declaring open war against the most powerful magical authority in North America."

"They declared war on us first," Luna pointed out with characteristic bluntness. "The question is whether we're going to keep pretending this is about individual conflicts instead of systematic oppression."

"What did you have in mind?" asked a new voice from the doorway. Eden turned to see Moira entering the war room, followed by three other Underground operatives whose arrival suggested important developments in their intelligence gathering.

"A demonstration," Eden replied, the idea crystallizing as she spoke. "Something public, undeniable, impossible to dismiss as the actions of isolated malcontents. Something that forces every practitioner in North America to acknowledge what the Council really represents."

The hunger in her chest roared with approval. This was what she'd been craving without knowing it—not just power, but the chance to use that power on a scale that would reshape everything.

"What kind of demonstration?" Moira asked, though her expression suggested both intrigue and concern in equal measure.

"The kind that shows them what we're capable of when we're not constrained by their arbitrary limitations," Eden said, her smile sharp and beautiful and utterly confident. "The kind that proves alternatives to their authority aren't just possible, but superior."

She moved to a section of the map that showed the Eastern Seaboard, her finger tracing a route that connected several major magical communities. "There's a gathering next month—the Autumn Convergence in Salem. Every significant magical family, organization, and independent practitioner on the East Coast will be there. Representatives from European magical communities, observers from the Pacific Coast councils, even some of the more reclusive solitary practitioners who rarely leave their territories."

"You want to recruit them," Marcus said, understanding immediately where her thoughts were leading.

"I want to offer them a choice," Eden corrected, though the distinction was becoming blurred in her mind. She didn't just want to offer choices— she wanted to shape them, control them, ensure that the only reasonable option was to submit to her vision of what the magical world should become. "Between the status quo and something better. Between serving a system that sees them as resources to be exploited and joining a movement that recognizes their inherent worth and potential."

"The risks would be enormous," Dr. Chen pointed out with academic precision. "The Council would interpret any public recruitment effort as an act of war. They'd respond with everything they have."

"Let them respond," Eden replied, her voice taking on harmonics that made the very air tremble with contained power. "I'm tired of tiptoeing around their sensibilities while they systematically murder anyone who disagrees with their policies. It's time to find out how many practitioners are ready to stand up and say 'enough.'"

The silence that followed was charged with possibility and danger in equal measure. What Eden was proposing would fundamentally alter the balance of power in magical society, forcing conflicts that had been simmering beneath the surface for decades into open confrontation.

It was also, Eden realized as she looked around the room at faces that showed both excitement and terror, exactly what needed to happen. The hunger that had been consuming her since her awakening had evolved into something far more ambitious than personal power—she wanted to remake the entire magical world, to claim dominion over every practitioner who might serve her purposes.

"The Salem Convergence is neutral ground," Moira said slowly, clearly working through the practical implications. "Ancient treaties, binding oaths, magical protections that make violence on the gathering grounds virtually impossible."

"Which means it's the perfect place to make a statement without worrying about immediate retaliation," Luna added with growing enthusiasm. "Whatever we do there, they'd have to respond afterward, on ground of our choosing."

"What kind of statement?" Marcus asked, his tactical mind already evaluating scenarios and contingencies.

Eden felt the familiar thrill of a plan coming together, pieces falling into place with the satisfying click of tumblers in a lock. The craving in her chest focused into laser intensity—she needed this victory, needed to prove her dominance on a scale that would satisfy the hunger consuming her.

"The kind that demonstrates what magical practice could look like without the Council's restrictions. Public displays of techniques they claim are too dangerous to teach, collaborative magic that shows what practitioners can accomplish when they're not competing for limited resources, innovations that prove their 'traditional methods' are holding everyone back."

"And if they try to stop us?" Dr. Chen asked.

"Then we prove that their authority depends on consent rather than inherent legitimacy," Eden replied, her power now blazing around her like a second sun. "And that consent can be withdrawn."

As the planning session continued deep into the night, Eden felt the familiar sensation of standing at the edge of something transformative. But this time, instead of simply accepting change as it happened to her, she was actively creating the conditions for the kind of transformation she wanted to see in the world.

The Council had spent centuries maintaining their authority through fear, manipulation, and the systematic elimination of alternatives. It was time to show the magical world that their supposed monopoly on legitimate power was nothing more than an elaborate lie supported by careful propaganda and strategic violence.

The hunger that had brought her to Ravenshollow was evolving into something far grander—the need to consume not just power, but entire systems of authority. She would reshape the magical world according to her vision, and everyone would have to choose whether to serve her willingly or be swept aside by forces they couldn't comprehend.

The revolution was no longer a distant possibility—it was an immediate necessity. And Eden Morrow was ready to lead it, to feed the cravings that demanded she become something far greater than any single practitioner had ever been.

The question was no longer whether she would succeed, but how much of the magical world would be left intact when her appetite was finally satisfied.

CHAPTER TWELVE

The Salem Gambit

Salem welcomed autumn with theatrical flair that only a place steeped in centuries of magical history could achieve.

Eden stood at her hotel window, watching leaves change colors in patterns too perfect for nature, observing tourists who had no idea they walked through streets where real magic had been practiced long before the witch trials gave the town its dark reputation. In the distance, Convergence Hall's spires rose like accusations against the steel-gray sky, Gothic architecture deliberately reminding all present of established magical authority's power and permanence.

The hunger that had been consuming her since her awakening had evolved into something razor-sharp and demanding. Today, that authority would face its first real challenge in centuries, and Eden would finally have the chance to feed on power on a scale that might actually satisfy her cravings.

"Second thoughts?" Kade asked, his reflection appearing in the glass as he approached with fluid grace that never failed to make her pulse quicken.

"Third and fourth thoughts," Eden admitted, turning to face him. He looked magnificent in formal robes—midnight blue silk embroidered with silver patterns that moved when she wasn't looking directly. The garments emphasized his classical features and lean strength, making him appear every inch the powerful sorcerer he was. "But not doubts. Never doubts."

"Good." His hands settled on her shoulders, warm and steadying despite the magnitude of what they were attempting. "Because in an hour, you're walking into a room full of North America's most powerful and conservative practitioners to tell them their worldview is wrong."

"When you put it like that, it sounds almost impossible."

"Almost impossible is your specialty," Kade replied, silver eyes warm with admiration and something deeper—promises of partnership and bonds transcending whatever challenges they faced. "Besides, you won't be facing them alone."

Through enhanced windows, Eden could see figures moving through Salem's historic streets—practitioners in everything from traditional robes to casual modern dress, all heading toward the same destination with purposeful strides marking them as people preparing for significant magical work. Some she recognized from Underground meetings, others were strangers who'd answered her call for a new kind of magical society.

The sight of them made her hunger spike with anticipation. So many practitioners, so much power, all gathered in one place where she could make her bid for dominance.

"How many?" she asked, though she'd been tracking invitation responses for weeks.

"Forty-seven confirmed allies," Luna's voice came from the communication array in the suite's living area. "Another dozen possibles attending but uncommitted to public support. And..." She paused, checking recent intelligence. "At least sixty Council loyalists, including faces I didn't expect."

"Anyone particularly concerning?" Marcus asked, looking up from Convergence Hall floor plans he'd been studying with siege warfare intensity.

"Magistrate Blackthorne, obviously. But also Aldric Ravencrest—the Council's chief enforcer, hasn't left his Adirondack stronghold in over a decade. If he's here, they're taking this very seriously."

Eden felt anticipation mixed with warranted apprehension. The Council bringing their most dangerous operatives to what was supposed to be a peaceful gathering suggested they were prepared for confrontation that could reshape magical society entirely.

Perfect. The bigger the audience, the more satisfying her inevitable victory would be.

"Perfect," she said, her smile sharp and confident. "I want them to understand exactly what they're dealing with."

The journey to Convergence Hall took them through Salem's historic district, past sites where mundane tourists photographed locations while completely unaware of their real magical significance. The Witch House, Old Burying Point, trial memorials—all hummed with accumulated power from centuries of practice, both public and hidden.

Convergence Hall itself took Eden's breath away and made her hunger roar with approval.

The building existed in multiple dimensions simultaneously, its architecture shifting between Gothic grandeur and impossible geometries depending on the observer's magical sensitivity. To mundane eyes, it appeared as an elegant conference center specializing in historical reenactments. To practitioners, it was a fortress of crystallized authority shaped by three centuries of magical politics and reinforced with accumulated power from every significant practitioner who'd ever entered.

Soon, all of that accumulated authority would belong to her.

"Impressive," Dr. Chen murmured as their group approached the main entrance, where formally dressed attendants checked invitations with efficiency suggesting they screened for more than proper documentation.

"Intimidating is the word I'd use," Luna replied, her punk aesthetic deliberately out of place among formal robes and traditional regalia. "They want everyone feeling small and insignificant before getting inside."

"Then they're going to be disappointed," Eden said, her eyes beginning to glow with familiar golden light as she approached the entrance. "I don't do small and insignificant anymore."

The moment she crossed the threshold, the building's accumulated power pressed against her enhanced awareness like physical weight—not hostile exactly, but evaluating, measuring, determining whether she belonged in a space designed to showcase established hierarchies' authority.

Eden pressed back with her own power, not aggressively but with quiet confidence of someone with every right to be exactly where she was. The building's resistance wavered, then dissolved entirely, as if her magical signature carried credentials superseding any formal invitation.

The sensation was intoxicating. Even the architecture recognized her dominance.

"Welcome to Convergence Hall," said a voice carrying undertones of surprise and possible respect. Eden turned to see an elderly man in formal robes approaching, weathered face showing dignity from decades managing complex political situations. "I'm Director Whitmore, and I must say, your magical signature is... remarkable."

"Thank you," Eden replied with graciousness suggesting complete comfort in such settings despite learning of their existence only months earlier. "I'm looking forward to participating in today's discussions."

"I imagine you are," Director Whitmore said, though his tone suggested less enthusiasm about her participation. "Your scheduled presentation is in the main auditorium at three o'clock. I trust you're prepared for... significant interest in your remarks."

"I'm prepared for whatever comes," Eden said simply, feeling the building itself hold its breath in anticipation.

The hours before her presentation passed in careful conversations and strategic positioning as allies and enemies maneuvered for optimal advantage. Eden moved through reception areas and meeting rooms with someone-who-belonged confidence, but her enhanced senses constantly evaluated threats, opportunities, and shifting power dynamics surrounding every interaction.

More than that, she was cataloging resources. Every practitioner she met was potential prey, a source of knowledge or power she might need to claim. The hunger in her chest sharpened with each introduction, each display of magical ability, each hint of expertise she didn't yet possess.

"Nervous yet?" Moira asked during a brief moment in a relatively private alcove, away from constant surveillance.

"Excited," Eden corrected, though she admitted the distinction was sometimes difficult. "This is what we've been building toward. Everything we've planned, every alliance forged, every risk taken—it all comes together this afternoon."

"And if it doesn't work?"

Eden looked over assembled practitioners, seeing not just individual faces but representation of an entire magical community told for centuries their only choice was between submission and elimination. Some appeared hopeful, others fearful, many simply curious about what notorious Eden Morrow might say about magical society's future.

But she saw something else too—weakness, complacency, practitioners who'd grown soft under the Council's protection. They would be easy to claim once she proved her superiority.

"Then we adapt and try something else," she said. "But it will work, Moira. It has to."

As afternoon progressed and presentation time approached, Eden felt familiar sensations of standing at transformation's edge. But this time, instead of change happening to her, she was actively creating conditions for the kind of transformation she wanted to see.

The main auditorium was packed beyond capacity when she took the stage, every seat filled and practitioners standing along walls and crowding aisles. Council loyalists clustered in front rows, faces carefully neutral but magical signatures radiating suspicion and barely controlled hostility. Her Underground allies scattered throughout the audience, positioned to provide support if things went badly but trying not to look like organized opposition.

In the back, almost hidden in shadows deeper than they should have been, Eden glimpsed figures whose presence made her enhanced senses recoil in alarm—and then surge forward with predatory interest. These weren't ordinary Council operatives—these were something else entirely, practitioners whose power felt ancient, hungry, utterly without mercy.

Potential rivals. Potential prey. The hunger in her chest focused on them with laser intensity.

"Ladies and gentlemen," Director Whitmore announced, his voice carrying clearly through enhanced acoustics, "please welcome Eden Morrow, heir to Ravenshollow Estate and... advocate for alternative approaches to magical practice."

Polite applause followed, containing undertones from genuine enthusiasm to barely concealed hostility, but Eden barely noticed. Her attention focused on the moment ahead, the opportunity to reshape magical society through words and demonstration rather than violence and coercion.

Though if violence became necessary, she was more than ready.

She stepped to the podium, looked out over hundreds of faces representing magical society's full spectrum, and felt her power respond to what she was attempting's magnitude.

"Three months ago," she began, her voice carrying new harmonics that made every person lean forward despite themselves, "I was living a mundane life in New York City, completely unaware magic existed or that I carried one of North American history's most powerful magical bloodlines."

A murmur ran through the audience—some surprised by her frank ignorance admission, others clearly skeptical that someone with so little formal training could pose real challenges to established authority.

"Today," Eden continued, her eyes beginning to glow with golden light that made the auditorium's magical fixtures respond with sympathetic luminance, "I stand before you as someone who's experienced both the wonder of awakening to magical potential and the horror of discovering what certain authorities will do to maintain their power monopoly."

The murmur grew louder, but Eden raised her hand and sound died instantly—not because she'd silenced it, but because her power's sheer presence made every person instinctively give complete attention.

The sensation was intoxicating. This was what she'd been craving—hundreds of magical practitioners hanging on her every word, reality itself bending to accommodate her will.

"I'm here to offer you a choice," she said, her voice now carrying enough power to make the building's foundations vibrate in sympathy. "Between a system that sees you as resources to be controlled and exploited, and a movement that recognizes your inherent worth and unlimited potential."

"And if we prefer established institutions' stability?" called out a voice from the front row—Magistrate Blackthorne, ice-blue eyes blazing with challenge and barely controlled fury.

Eden's smile was radiant, dangerous, full of promise. "Then you're welcome to keep them, Magistrate. But you're not welcome to force that choice on the rest of us."

The response was immediate and electric. Half the audience erupted in applause that shook the auditorium's enhanced architecture, while the other half responded with hostile energy suggesting violence barely restrained by ancient treaties making Convergence Hall neutral ground.

Eden felt power flow through her as she absorbed the emotional energy of hundreds of practitioners. Their fear, their hope, their anger—all of it fed the hunger that had been consuming her since her awakening.

"The question isn't whether change is coming," Eden continued, her power blazing around her like visible fire. "Change is here. The question is whether you'll help shape it or be shaped by it."

She gestured, and reality bent around her like willing clay. The air above the auditorium filled with demonstrations of techniques that shouldn't have been possible—collaborative spells drawing power from multiple practitioners simultaneously, innovations combining different magical traditions in ways established schools claimed were impossible, applications transcending every limitation the Council insisted were necessary for public safety.

But more than that, she was drawing power from every person in the audience. Their awe, their fear, their desperate hunger for something greater than what they'd been offered—all of it flowed into her like wine, making her stronger, more magnificent, more worthy of the dominion she was claiming.

"This is what we could achieve," Eden said, her voice carrying over gasps and exclamations, "if we stopped letting fear dictate possibility's boundaries."

The silence that followed was profound, charged with understanding that they'd witnessed something that would reshape their understanding of magical potential forever.

Then Magistrate Blackthorne rose, her power flaring around her like winter given form.

"Impressive theatrics," she said, her voice carrying enough authority to make several practitioners step backward involuntarily. "But power without wisdom, innovation without restraint, change without considering consequences—these lead to chaos, not progress."

"And who decides what constitutes wisdom?" Eden asked, descending from the podium to face the Magistrate directly. "Who determines which innovations are acceptable? Who gets to define which consequences matter?"

"Those with experience and judgment to make such determinations responsibly."

"You mean those with the most to lose if the current system changes."

The confrontation between them now drew power from everyone in the auditorium, magical energy building to levels that made the air itself seem combustible. Eden could feel the moment balanced on a knife's edge— one wrong word, one careless gesture, and the peaceful gathering would explode into magical warfare that could level city blocks.

More importantly, she could feel power flowing toward her from every direction. The audience's attention, their emotional investment, their desperate need for something greater than what they'd been offered—all of it was feeding her, making her stronger, more magnificent.

"Choose," she said, addressing not just Magistrate Blackthorne but every practitioner in the auditorium. Her voice carried harmonics that seemed to rewrite reality around them, making her words feel inevitable, necessary, the only reasonable option. "Continue accepting limitations imposed by people who profit from your compliance, or discover what you're truly capable of when free to pursue your full potential."

"And if chaos results from that freedom?" Blackthorne demanded.

Eden's smile was beautiful, terrible, absolutely certain. "Then we'll deal with chaos created by our own choices rather than order imposed by someone else's fear."

The applause that erupted was thunderous, drowning out whatever response the Magistrate might have offered. But Eden barely heard it—her attention focused on the power flowing into her from hundreds of practitioners, their hope and fear and desperate hunger for transformation.

She was feeding on them, consuming their emotional energy, their magical potential, their very essence. Not completely—that would have been noticed—but enough to satisfy the craving that had been eating her alive since her awakening.

The presentation was over, but the real feast was just beginning.

As practitioners approached her afterward—some seeking alliance, others demanding answers, all of them drawn by power they couldn't resist—Eden felt the hunger in her chest roar with satisfaction.

This was what she'd been craving all along. Not just magical ability, not just political influence, but the chance to consume everything the magical world had to offer. Every practitioner who pledged themselves to her cause, every enemy who opposed her vision, every neutral party who thought they could remain uninvolved—all of them were potential sources of power, knowledge, essence she could claim.

The revolution she'd started was really just the beginning of a much larger feast. And Eden Morrow was discovering that her appetite was far larger than anyone—including herself—had ever imagined.

The question was no longer whether she would reshape the magical world according to her vision, but how much of it would survive the process of feeding her ever-growing hunger.

The Collector's Gambit

The invitation arrived that evening, written in blood-red ink on parchment that felt disturbingly warm and smelled of roses left too long in darkness.

> *My Dear Lady Morrow,*
>
> *Your performance this afternoon was… illuminating. I would be honored if you would join me for dinner tonight to discuss certain opportunities that might interest someone of your remarkable talents.*
>
> *I shall send a car at eight o'clock. Do try not to disappoint me by refusing—I so rarely encounter specimens of your caliber, and I would hate for our introduction to be… postponed indefinitely.*
>
> *With great anticipation, Cordelia Blackwood The Collector*

The hunger that had been partially satisfied by her performance earlier roared back to life at the veiled threat. Eden craved the confrontation this represented—another chance to prove her dominance, to claim victory over someone who dared to see her as prey rather than predator.

"The Collector," Kade said when Eden showed him the invitation, his face paling in a way that made her enhanced senses tingle with alarm. "I'd hoped the stories were exaggerations, but if she's here…"

"What stories?" Eden asked, though the parchment's pulsing heartbeat suggested she might not want to know.

"Cordelia Blackwood collects powerful magical practitioners the way some people collect rare books or fine wines," Marcus replied grimly, looking up from defensive preparations he'd been making throughout their suite. "She keeps them in her private estate, beautiful and compliant and utterly devoted to her will."

"Keeps them how?" Eden felt ice form in her veins at the casual description of what sounded remarkably like slavery—though underneath the revulsion was something else. Curiosity. Professional interest in techniques she might be able to adapt for her own purposes.

"Various methods. Magical compulsion, psychological manipulation, gradual erosion of will until her... guests... can't imagine wanting anything except her approval and affection." Kade's silver eyes were dark with something that looked remarkably like fear. "Some of her collection have been with her for decades, maybe centuries. They're perfectly happy, perfectly content, and perfectly incapable of independent thought."

Eden stared at the invitation, feeling power stir in response to her growing fury—and fascination. The parchment began to smoke where her fingers touched it, blood-red ink shifting and flowing as if trying to escape her magical influence.

The techniques Cordelia used sounded remarkably similar to what Eden had been unconsciously developing—the way she'd been drawing power from the audience at her presentation, feeding on their emotional energy, subtly influencing their thoughts to make her words seem more compelling. The difference was scale and refinement.

"She's not getting within a hundred miles of me," she said, her voice taking on harmonics that made every magical implement in the suite hum with sympathetic vibrations.

"Unfortunately, I don't think we have that luxury," Dr. Chen said from her position at the communication array, expression grim as she reviewed latest intelligence reports. "Our sources indicate Cordelia arrived in Salem with a significant entourage—not just personal attendants, but practitioners whose magical signatures suggest they're operating under some form of compulsion."

"Her existing collection," Luna added with disgust despite her usual irreverent demeanor. "She brought them as a demonstration of what she's capable of, probably hoping to intimidate you into compliance."

"It's not going to work," Eden said flatly. "I don't care how powerful she is or how many people she's brainwashed—I'm not becoming anyone's pet sorceress."

But even as she spoke, part of her mind was analyzing what she'd learned. Cordelia had managed to maintain control over dozens of powerful practitioners for decades. The techniques required for that level of sustained domination were exactly what Eden needed to master if she was going to reshape the magical world according to her vision.

"The problem," Moira said quietly from her position by the window, where she'd been monitoring magical activity in the streets below, "is that refusing her invitation might not be an option. Cordelia Blackwood doesn't make requests—she makes statements of intent. If you don't go to her willingly..."

"She'll come to me," Eden finished, understanding immediately why everyone looked so concerned. "And if she does that, other people could get caught in whatever confrontation results."

The silence that followed was heavy with implications. Eden looked around the suite at faces showing varying degrees of fear, determination, and calculation, and felt familiar responsibility weight settling on her shoulders.

These people had committed themselves to her cause, put their lives at risk to support her vision of what magical society could become.

More than that, they were resources she'd invested considerable effort in acquiring. She couldn't afford to lose them to some collector's whims.

"I'll go," she decided, ignoring immediate protests from everyone in the room. "But not alone, and not unprepared."

"Eden, this is exactly what she wants," Kade said, his voice tight with barely controlled panic. "Cordelia specializes in isolating her targets, getting them away from support networks so she can work on them without interference."

"Then we don't let her isolate me." Eden moved to the mirror dominating one wall of the suite, studying her reflection and noting changes that had occurred since her magical awakening. Her eyes held flecks of gold that pulsed with their own inner light, her hair carried threads of silver that caught illumination from sources that didn't exist in normal reality, and her skin seemed to glow with power becoming harder to conceal with each passing day.

She looked like someone who could face down a collector of magical practitioners and emerge victorious—and possibly learn some useful techniques in the process.

"What did you have in mind?" Marcus asked, his tactical instincts clearly engaged despite obvious reservations about the entire plan.

"Something Cordelia won't expect—honesty, directness, and enough backup power to make it clear that I'm not as vulnerable as she assumes." Eden turned from the mirror to face the assembled group, expression determined despite what she was contemplating's magnitude. "She wants to meet the notorious Eden Morrow? Fine. Let's give her a demonstration of exactly what she's trying to collect."

The preparations took two hours and involved magical techniques that pushed the boundaries of what most practitioners considered possible. Working together, Eden and her allies created connection spells that would allow them to share power across significant distances, communication enchantments that would function even if she was transported to different dimensions, and emergency protocols that would bring immediate rescue if the situation deteriorated beyond salvage.

But it was the personal preparations that proved most intriguing.

As Eden selected jewelry serving double duty as both adornment and magical amplification, she found herself genuinely curious about what Cordelia had accomplished. The necklace she chose was a complex piece of silver and sapphires that had belonged to previous Virelli women, each stone holding accumulated power from decades of use. The earrings were more subtle but no less potent—tiny diamonds that could store and release energy in precisely controlled bursts.

"You're sure about this?" Kade asked as Eden fastened a bracelet containing enough stored power to level city blocks if properly deployed.

"I'm sure about protecting the people I care about," Eden replied, though that wasn't the complete truth. "I'm sure about not letting some ancient parasite think she can intimidate me into submission. I'm sure about making it clear that the Underground isn't helpless against practitioners who abuse their authority."

What she didn't say was that she was also sure about her curiosity. Cordelia had developed techniques for controlling other practitioners that Eden desperately wanted to understand. If she could learn those methods, adapt them, improve upon them...

The car that arrived at precisely eight o'clock was a work of art—a vintage Rolls-Royce modified with magical enhancements that made it more like a mobile fortress than a luxury vehicle. The driver was a young man whose blank expression and mechanical movements suggested he was operating under some form of compulsion, but his magical signature showed traces of power that would have been formidable before Cordelia got her hands on him.

"Another member of her collection," Eden murmured to Kade as they settled into the car's luxurious interior. "She brought him along to demonstrate what I have to look forward to if I don't cooperate."

The journey through Salem's historic streets took them past sites where real magic had been practiced for centuries, but Eden barely noticed familiar landmarks. Her attention was focused on the magical signatures she could sense throughout the city—some familiar from the Underground network, others carrying Council authority's distinctive resonance, and underneath it all, something vast and hungry and utterly inhuman that made her enhanced senses recoil in instinctive alarm.

And respond with predatory interest.

"She's not entirely human," Eden said as they turned onto a road leading away from the city center toward what appeared to be an abandoned industrial district. "Whatever Cordelia Blackwood was originally, centuries of collecting other people's power has changed her into something else entirely."

"Does that change your approach?"

"It makes me more determined to succeed," Eden replied, her eyes beginning to glow with golden radiance that made the car's magical enhancements respond with sympathetic luminescence. "Predators like her only understand one language—superior force applied with absolute conviction."

But underneath her confidence was genuine curiosity. What had Cordelia become? How had she managed to sustain herself by consuming other practitioners' essence? What techniques had she developed that Eden might be able to learn?

The building they stopped in front of looked like an ordinary warehouse from the outside, but Eden's enhanced vision could perceive layers of concealment and protection hiding its true nature. This wasn't just a meeting place—it was a fortress designed to contain and control magical practitioners who might resist Cordelia's influence.

The interior of the warehouse had been transformed into something belonging in a different century entirely—elegant furnishings that wouldn't have looked out of place in a European palace, artwork probably stolen from museums decades earlier, and an atmosphere of refined luxury that couldn't quite disguise the underlying wrongness permeating everything.

But it was the people that made Eden's blood sing with hunger.

They stood around the main space's perimeter like living statues—men and women of various ages and backgrounds, all strikingly beautiful, all wearing expressions of serene contentment that didn't reach their eyes. Their magical signatures showed traces of formidable power, but power that had been carefully channeled, controlled, directed toward serving purposes that had nothing to do with their original intentions or desires.

The sight of them made Eden's craving spike with professional interest. This was what perfect control looked like—practitioners whose very essence had been reshaped to serve another's will. She needed to understand how it was done.

"My collection," said a voice like honey poured over broken glass. "Aren't they magnificent?"

Cordelia Blackwood emerged from shadows at the warehouse's far end, and Eden's first glimpse was like looking at winter given human form. She appeared to be in her forties but moved with fluid grace of someone who'd learned to inhabit multiple bodies over centuries. Her auburn hair fell in perfect waves to her waist, her clothing was simple but exquisite, and her amber eyes held depths speaking of knowledge acquired through methods that didn't bear close examination.

But more than that, Eden could sense the power radiating from her—not just magical ability, but something else. Accumulated essence, consciousness structures that had been absorbed and integrated, personalities that had been consumed and digested until only their most useful elements remained.

It was beautiful. Terrifying. Absolutely fascinating.

"Lady Morrow," Cordelia continued, approaching with confidence of someone who'd never encountered a situation she couldn't ultimately control. "You're even more striking than I'd been led to believe."

"Ms. Blackwood," Eden replied, noting how her own voice seemed to make several collection members stir restlessly, as if some deep part of their consciousness recognized something in her that called to their suppressed independence. "Thank you for the invitation, though I have to say, your hospitality has some disturbing undertones."

Cordelia's laugh was like silver bells touched with frost. "Direct. I appreciate that in a potential acquisition. Most practitioners try to hide their true nature behind politeness and social conventions. You, however, seem refreshingly honest about what you are."

"And what am I?"

"The most powerful sorceress born in centuries, completely untrained in magical society's subtle arts, operating without proper guidance or oversight." Cordelia's gaze traveled over Eden with a connoisseur's assessment examining particularly fine art. "In other words, exactly what I've been waiting for."

Eden felt her power respond to the predatory hunger in the other woman's voice, golden light beginning to flicker around her hands like controlled lightning. Several collection members took involuntary steps backward, their compelled serenity cracking slightly as they felt magic's presence that operated according to different rules than what they'd been taught to expect.

The hunger in Eden's chest sharpened into something that demanded immediate attention. She needed to understand Cordelia's techniques, needed to learn how such perfect control was achieved and maintained.

"I'm afraid you're going to be disappointed," Eden said, her smile sharp and beautiful and utterly without compromise. "I'm not interested in becoming anyone's pet sorceress."

"Oh, my dear," Cordelia replied, her amber eyes gleaming with anticipation and something darker, "you haven't heard my offer yet."

The offer, when it came, was everything Eden had expected and nothing she could have prepared for.

"You see slavery where I see sanctuary," Cordelia said, settling into a chair that materialized from shadows as if the warehouse itself was reshaping reality to accommodate her desires. Her amber eyes were gentle, sincere. "Miranda came to me broken—suffragette ideals shattered by a world that would never change. Charles was dying from magical cancer, eaten alive by power he couldn't control. I saved them from despair, from pain, from the crushing weight of making choices in a universe that punishes every mistake."

She touched Miranda's cheek with genuine affection. "Look at her peace, Eden. When did you last sleep without nightmares? When did you last wake without the weight of others' expectations crushing you? I offer rest from the burden of consciousness itself."

Eden remained standing, her power crackling around her like visible electricity as she studied Cordelia's collection members. Up close, she could see what the offer had cost them—their eyes held emptiness that came from centuries of having every decision made for them, every desire channeled through someone else's will.

But she could also see the techniques involved. Subtle magical bindings that rewrote neural pathways, psychological conditioning reinforced through mystical compulsion, gradual erosion of individual identity until only compliance remained.

It was masterful work. Eden found herself genuinely impressed by the sophistication involved.

"At what price?" Eden asked, though she was increasingly certain she already knew the answer.

"Service, naturally. Dedication to pursuits greater than individual ambition." Cordelia gestured gracefully toward her assembled collection, and Eden noticed how they all turned slightly toward their mistress, like flowers tracking the sun. "These lovely people have found perfect contentment serving my research, my experiments, my various projects. They want for nothing, fear nothing, regret nothing."

"Because they can't want or fear or regret anything you haven't approved of first."

Cordelia's smile was radiant and completely without warmth. "Exactly. Freedom from the burden of independent choice, from uncertainty's anxiety, from the pain of making mistakes that can't be undone. I offer purpose, direction, and the kind of perfect happiness most people never achieve despite decades of struggle."

Eden looked more closely at the collection, using her enhanced senses to perceive magical bindings holding them in thrall. What she found was both more subtle and more horrifying than she'd expected—not crude domination, but careful erosion of will over months or years until the victims couldn't imagine wanting anything except their captor's approval.

The techniques were elegant, refined, absolutely brilliant in their execution. Eden felt the hunger in her chest roar with desperate need—she had to learn these methods, had to understand how such perfect control was achieved.

"How long?" she asked, focusing on a woman who appeared to be in her thirties but whose magical signature carried traces of power speaking of much longer experience.

"Miranda has been with me for... oh, nearly eight decades now," Cordelia replied with casual affection of someone discussing a favorite pet. "She was quite rebellious initially—a suffragette, if you can imagine, convinced she could change the world through political action rather than magical superiority. It took almost two years to help her understand how much happier she could be serving more elevated purposes."

The woman—Miranda—smiled serenely at mention of her name, but Eden caught a flicker of something in her eyes that might have been recognition, a momentary crack in perfect contentment suggesting some part of her original personality still existed beneath layers of compulsion.

Eden felt her power surge in response to the casual way Cordelia described decades of enslavement, golden light flaring around her like a second skin. The warehouse's magical fixtures began to resonate with her emotional state, humming with harmonics that made several collection members press their hands to their ears.

But underneath the righteous anger was something else—professional admiration. What Cordelia had accomplished was extraordinary, requiring levels of skill and knowledge that Eden desperately craved.

"I'm not interested," she said, her voice carrying enough authority to make the building's foundations vibrate in sympathy.

"Of course you are," Cordelia replied, apparently unperturbed by the raw power display. "You simply haven't considered all the implications yet. Think about what you could accomplish with unlimited time and resources, Eden. Think about the knowledge you could accumulate, the innovations you could develop, the changes you could implement in magical society."

"Under your direction and according to your priorities."

"Under my guidance, certainly. But I'm not unreasonable—talented acquisitions are always given considerable latitude in pursuing their interests, as long as those interests don't conflict with the greater good."

"Whose definition of the greater good?"

Cordelia's laugh was like breaking crystal. "Mine, naturally. Who else has the experience and perspective necessary to make such determinations?"

Eden felt something snap inside her chest—not breaking, but settling into place like the final piece of a puzzle she'd been unconsciously assembling since arriving at Ravenshollow. This was what she'd been preparing for without knowing it, what all her training and growth and awakening had been leading toward.

The hunger that had been consuming her since her awakening suddenly found perfect focus. She didn't want to destroy Cordelia—she wanted to consume her, to absorb her knowledge, to claim her collection and improve upon her techniques.

"No," she said, and the word carried such finality that several collection members actually took steps toward her, as if some deep part of their consciousness recognized it as the sound of genuine freedom.

"I beg your pardon?"

"I said no. I'm not interested in your offer, your collection, or your version of the greater good." Eden's power began to manifest more dramatically, reality bending around her like willing clay. "What I am interested in is giving your collection a choice they haven't had in decades—and learning everything you know about controlling other practitioners."

"Impossible," Cordelia snapped, her perfect composure finally showing cracks. "The bindings I've placed are absolute, unbreakable, reinforced by years of conditioning and magical enhancement—"

"Reinforced by despair," Eden corrected, advancing toward the nearest collection member—Miranda, the former suffragette whose eyes had shown that flicker of recognition. "By isolation, by gradual erosion of hope until your victims couldn't imagine any alternative to the prison you've created for them."

She reached out with abilities she'd only recently discovered she possessed, not attacking Cordelia's bindings directly but offering something else— connection, recognition, the reminder that choice was always possible for those brave enough to claim it.

But more than that, she was analyzing the bindings themselves, studying their structure, understanding their function. Knowledge flowed into her consciousness like wine as she examined decades of sophisticated magical work.

"But despair isn't permanent," Eden continued, her voice now carrying harmonics that seemed to resonate in dimensions most people couldn't perceive. "And neither is any prison built from someone else's will."

Miranda's eyes widened as Eden's power touched the magical constraints that had defined her existence for eight decades. For a moment, the two women stared at each other across the space between captivity and freedom, and Eden felt the exact instant when decades of conditioning cracked and fell away like chains made of glass.

"I..." Miranda's voice was hoarse, as if she hadn't used it for her own purposes in longer than she could remember. "I remember who I was. Before. I remember wanting things, choosing things, believing I could make a difference."

"You still can," Eden said gently, extending her power to touch each collection member in turn. "All of you still can."

The effect was immediate and overwhelming. Decades of suppressed personality began reasserting itself as Eden's influence spread through the warehouse, years of accumulated resentment and thwarted desire emerging from whatever psychological depths Cordelia's conditioning had buried them in.

But even as she freed them, Eden was learning. Each binding she dissolved taught her something new about the techniques involved, the psychological mechanisms that made such control possible, the subtle ways consciousness could be shaped and reshaped to serve another's purposes.

"Stop," Cordelia commanded, her own power flaring to life around her like winter given form. "You don't understand what you're doing—these people need guidance, structure, purpose greater than their individual desires—"

"They need freedom," Eden replied, her power now blazing around her like a second sun. "The same thing every conscious being needs—the right to make their own choices, even if those choices lead to mistakes, pain, or uncertainty."

"You're destroying decades of careful work—"

"I'm correcting decades of systematic abuse while learning everything you know about controlling other practitioners."

The confrontation between them now drew power from sources transcending normal magical practice—not just their individual abilities, but fundamental forces governing concepts like freedom and captivity, choice and compulsion, individual will versus imposed order.

Around them, the warehouse began to transform as collection members reclaimed aspects of their original personalities. Charles, the former Council enforcer, was staring at his hands as if seeing them for the first time in forty years. A young man who appeared to be in his twenties but whose magical signature suggested much greater age was laughing and crying simultaneously as memories of a life before Cordelia reasserted themselves.

But Eden's attention was focused on something else—the flow of knowledge and power she was absorbing from Cordelia's techniques. Every binding she dissolved, every mind she freed, taught her more about the sophisticated methods required to control other practitioners. She was learning faster than she'd ever learned anything, consuming decades of accumulated expertise in minutes.

"This is chaos," Cordelia snarled, her carefully maintained facade cracking to reveal something ancient and hungry and utterly without mercy. "You're offering them pain, uncertainty, the possibility of failure and regret—"

"I'm offering them life," Eden said simply. "Real life, with all its complications and risks and possibilities for growth. Not the perfect stagnation you've been providing."

Cordelia raised her hands, and Eden felt the attack beginning—not physical violence, but something far more intimate and dangerous. The Collector was trying to do to her what she had done to dozens of others over centuries, eroding her will gradually, planting suggestions that would eventually bloom into absolute obedience.

It might have worked on someone else.

Eden smiled and opened herself completely to Cordelia's influence, allowing the other woman's power to flow into her consciousness without resistance. But instead of being overwhelmed by superior force, Eden found herself analyzing the techniques being used against her, understanding the psychological mechanisms that made such control possible, learning methods she could potentially use to heal others who had suffered similar violations.

And more than that—she was feeding. Cordelia's accumulated knowledge, her centuries of experience, her understanding of consciousness manipulation—all of it flowed into Eden like a banquet she'd been craving without knowing it.

"Impossible," Cordelia breathed, her attack faltering as she realized it was being absorbed rather than resisted. "No one has that level of natural immunity—"

"I don't have immunity," Eden replied, her power now encompassing not just herself but every person in the warehouse. "I have something better— the absolute certainty that my choices are my own, my will is inviolate, and my purpose is to ensure that others have the same protection while learning everything you know about controlling those who don't."

She gestured, and the warehouse exploded with golden light that seemed to burn away everything false, everything imposed, everything that existed only because someone else had decided it should. When the radiance faded, Cordelia's perfect sanctuary had been transformed into something resembling a rehabilitation center—comfortable spaces for people recovering from trauma, resources for rebuilding interrupted lives, and most importantly, exits that were completely unguarded.

But more than that, Eden had claimed something far more valuable than just physical victory. Cordelia's knowledge, her techniques, her centuries of accumulated expertise—all of it now resided in Eden's consciousness, ready to be studied, refined, improved upon.

"Go," Eden said to the collection members, who were looking around with the dazed wonder of people seeing sunlight after years of darkness. "Go wherever you want, be whoever you choose to be, make whatever mistakes you need to make to remember what it feels like to be alive."

Most of them fled immediately, decades of suppressed survival instincts finally given permission to assert themselves. But a few lingered, looking at Eden with something that might have been gratitude or worship or simple human recognition.

"Thank you," Miranda said, her voice stronger now, carrying traces of fierce determination that had once driven her to fight for women's suffrage. "I had forgotten what it felt like to have my own thoughts, my own dreams. How can I repay you?"

"By living," Eden replied simply. "By making choices, even when they're difficult. By remembering that freedom isn't a gift someone gives you—it's something you claim and defend every single day."

As the last former collection members disappeared into Salem night, Eden turned her attention back to Cordelia, who was standing amid her sanctuary's ruins with such rage and loss that it almost bordered on tragic.

"Centuries of work," Cordelia whispered, her amber eyes blazing with fury that made air around her shimmer with heat. "Decades of careful cultivation, perfect specimens serving purposes greater than their individual limitations—and you've destroyed it all in minutes."

"I've given them back their lives," Eden corrected, though she found herself studying the other woman with something that might have been pity. "The question is what you're going to do with the rest of yours."

"What I'm going to do," Cordelia said, her voice taking on harmonics suggesting she was drawing power from sources that should have been forbidden to any sane practitioner, "is demonstrate why collecting dangerous specimens sometimes requires more... permanent solutions."

The attack that followed was unlike anything Eden had experienced—not dream walker's psychic intrusion or Seraphina's political manipulation, but something striking at identity's very foundations. Cordelia was trying to unmake her, to convince reality that Eden Morrow had never existed, that her memories and relationships and accumulated experiences were nothing more than elaborate delusions.

For a terrifying moment, Eden felt herself wavering between existence and nonexistence, caught in space between what was real and what Cordelia's will was trying to impose on the universe.

Then she felt something else—a connection transcending physical distance through her bond with Kade, her ties to Ravenshollow, the network of allies who'd committed themselves to her cause. Through these connections, Eden found anchor points no amount of reality manipulation could sever.

But more than that, she had Cordelia's own knowledge to draw upon. The techniques the Collector had tried to use against her were now part of Eden's repertoire, and she understood exactly how to counter them.

"You made a mistake," she said, her voice growing stronger as she drew power from sources Cordelia couldn't perceive or counter. "You assumed I was like your collection—isolated, dependent on a single source of identity. But I'm not alone, and I'm not dependent on anyone else's definition of who I am."

She reached out through connections binding her to the Underground network, to practitioners who'd committed themselves to changing magical society, to everyone who'd ever been told they were too dangerous to be allowed to develop their full potential.

The response was immediate and overwhelming—power flowed back through channels Cordelia's centuries of experience had never taught her to recognize, strength that came not from domination but from voluntary alliance and shared purpose.

"Impossible," Cordelia gasped, her reality-unmaking attack crumbling under sheer weight of collective will Eden was channeling. "No individual practitioner can command that much cooperative power—"

"You're right," Eden agreed, her form now blazing with light from dozens of different sources. "No individual practitioner can. But I'm not just an individual anymore—I'm part of something larger, something that exists because people chose to support it rather than because they were forced to submit to it."

She gestured, and power she was channeling focused on Cordelia with surgical precision. Not seeking to destroy or control, but to offer the same choice she'd given collection members—the opportunity to remember what it felt like to exist for her own purposes rather than as extension of her hunger for dominance over others.

For a moment, something flickered in Cordelia's amber eyes that might have been recognition, vulnerability, memory of a time when she'd been content to exist without needing to possess everyone around her.

Then the moment passed, buried under centuries of habit and accumulated choices that couldn't be undone.

"I am what I chose to become," Cordelia said with dignity that was both admirable and tragic. "And I will not be unmade by someone who doesn't understand survival's necessities in a world offering only the choice between predator and prey."

"There are other choices," Eden said, though she could see Cordelia was too deeply committed to her path to consider alternatives. "There always have been."

"Perhaps. But I made mine long ago, and I will live—or die—with the consequences."

She began to fade, not fleeing but withdrawing to whatever sanctuary she maintained for herself when the world proved less accommodating than she preferred. But before disappearing entirely, she turned back to Eden with an expression holding both respect and warning.

"This isn't over," she said. "You've made enemies today who have resources and patience extending far beyond what you've encountered. They will come for you, Eden Morrow, and when they do, they won't make the mistake of underestimating you again."

"Let them come," Eden replied, her power still blazing around her like a beacon visible from dimensions most people couldn't imagine. "I'll be ready."

As Cordelia vanished into whatever retreat she'd prepared, Eden found herself alone in a warehouse already beginning to return to its mundane appearance. The magical enhancements were fading, elegant furnishings were dissolving back into ordinary industrial equipment, and atmosphere of refined menace was giving way to simple emptiness.

But the victory felt different from her previous confrontations with Council representatives. This time, she hadn't just defended herself or demonstrated her abilities—she had actively freed people held captive for decades, given them back choices stolen through manipulation and psychological abuse.

And more than that, she had claimed something invaluable—Cordelia's knowledge, her techniques, her understanding of how consciousness could be shaped and controlled. All of it now resided in Eden's mind, ready to be studied, refined, adapted to her own purposes.

The hunger that had been consuming her since her awakening was finally beginning to be satisfied in ways she'd never imagined. She didn't just want power anymore—she wanted everything. Every technique, every method, every secret that could help her reshape the magical world according to her vision.

And now she had the tools to begin that reshaping in earnest.

CHAPTER FOURTEEN

The Council's Response

The attack came at dawn, three days after Eden's confrontation with Cordelia, when mist still clung to Salem's historic streets like smoke from centuries-old fires.

Eden woke to alarms that shouldn't have existed—not mechanical security systems, but something primal, warnings resonating in the deepest parts of her magical consciousness. The hunger that had become her constant companion twisted into something sharp and defensive, her power responding to threats she couldn't yet identify.

But underneath the alarm was anticipation. She craved this confrontation, needed to prove her dominance against whatever force dared to challenge her growing authority.

Before she was fully awake, she was already rolling from bed and channeling power, silk pajamas seeming inadequate for whatever confrontation awaited. Through suite's enhanced windows, she could see figures moving through pre-dawn darkness—not careful stealth of Underground operatives or obvious authority of local law enforcement, but something else entirely. They moved with military precision, their magical signatures coordinated in ways that spoke of extensive training and absolute commitment to their mission.

"Council enforcement teams," Kade said grimly, appearing beside her with weapons that definitely hadn't been part of his usual traveling equipment.

"Full tactical deployment, probably thirty or forty practitioners, all specifically trained for this kind of operation."

"What kind of operation?" Eden asked, though she suspected the answer would be exactly what she feared.

"The kind designed to eliminate threats to established order with maximum efficiency and minimum political complications." His silver eyes were dark with fury and something that might have been fear—not for himself, but for her. "They're not here to arrest you, Eden. They're here to end you."

The craving in her chest crystallized into perfect focus. These people had come to her territory, threatened her allies, dared to challenge her authority. They would learn what happened when they underestimated her.

The first attack came as precisely coordinated assault on the building's structural integrity—not crude demolition, but surgical magical strikes designed to bring down the entire hotel while making it appear as if architectural failure rather than supernatural violence was responsible.

Eden reached out with abilities that had been growing stronger every day since her awakening, not just her individual power but her connection to the network of practitioners who'd chosen to support her vision. The building's collapse stopped mid-destruction, debris hanging suspended in mid-air as if frozen by will alone.

But she wasn't content with simply preventing the attack—she was interested in sending a message.

With power that came from dozens of allied practitioners working in concert, she began to reconstruct the hotel around them—not just repairing damage, but improving on original design. The mundane structure became something existing partially in normal reality and partially in dimensions where different rules applied, a fortress that could accommodate magical warfare without endangering innocent people nearby.

The sensation of reshaping reality itself made her hunger roar with satisfaction. This was what she'd been craving—power on a scale that could remake the world according to her vision.

"Impressive," said a voice carrying authority so vast it made the transformed building tremble in response. "But ultimately futile."

The speaker materialized on suite's balcony—not through any door or window, but by stepping out of shadows that definitely hadn't been deep enough to conceal a human figure moments before. He was tall, elegantly dressed, with silver hair and eyes like winter storms, and power radiated from him with casual intensity suggesting centuries of accumulated knowledge and absolutely no moral constraints about how that knowledge should be applied.

"High Magistrate Aldric Ravencrest," Kade said, his voice tight with recognition and what might have been old hatred. "I should have known they'd send you personally."

"Mr. Virelli." Ravencrest's smile was cultured and cold and utterly without warmth. "Still playing guardian to bloodlines that should have been eliminated generations ago, I see. Though I suppose I should thank you—your success in awakening the Morrow girl's abilities saved us considerable effort in locating and harvesting her potential."

Eden felt power surge in response to the casual way he discussed her as if she were a resource to be exploited rather than a person with agency and rights. Golden light began to flicker around her hands, and she noticed with satisfaction that several pieces of furniture in the suite began to crack under pressure of her emotional response.

The craving in her chest sharpened into something that demanded immediate satisfaction through violence. This man had come here to destroy her, to eliminate her as a threat to his organization's authority. She would make him understand exactly what kind of mistake that was.

"Careful, child," Ravencrest continued, apparently unimpressed by the display of raw magical force. "Power without proper understanding is dangerous—to yourself and to everyone around you. Consider what happened to your mother when she chose defiance over cooperation."

The words hit Eden like physical blows, and she felt something snap inside her chest—not breaking, but settling into place like the final piece of a puzzle she'd been unconsciously assembling since arriving at Ravenshollow.

"You killed her," she said, her voice taking on harmonics that made the transformed hotel's magical fixtures hum with sympathetic vibrations. "The car accident—it wasn't an accident at all."

"Your mother was offered the same choice you're being offered now," Ravencrest replied with casual indifference of someone discussing weather rather than murder. "Cooperation with established authority, or elimination as a threat to magical society's stability. She chose poorly."

"She chose freedom over slavery."

"She chose chaos over order, and paid the appropriate price." His winter-storm eyes held no remorse, no recognition that he was discussing the death of someone's beloved parent. "Her mistake was believing that individual conscience was more important than collective security."

Eden felt her power building to levels that made air around them shimmer with heat, but before she could respond, Kade moved.

The explosion of force that erupted from him was unlike anything Eden had seen from him before—not controlled demonstrations he'd shown her during training, but raw protective fury that made reality itself recoil. Furniture didn't just crack under pressure—it disintegrated, reformed, became something that existed primarily as weaponized intent.

The sight of him unleashing his full power in her defense made the hunger in her chest roar with possessive satisfaction. This was what she'd been craving—someone strong enough to match her, powerful enough to fight beside her against whatever enemies dared to challenge their dominion.

"Touch her," Kade snarled, his cultured voice carrying undertones of violence that belonged to something far older and more dangerous than his apparent age suggested, "and I'll show you why the last Virelli guardian earned the name 'Soulreaper.'"

The casual threat of absolute violence in defense of her made Eden's knees weak for reasons that had nothing to do with fear. The way he'd positioned himself between her and Ravencrest, the way his power had responded not to direct threat but to simple possibility that someone might harm her—it was possessive and protective and utterly without compromise.

"Ah," Ravencrest said, his smile widening with something that might have been amusement. "The guardian bond has evolved beyond mere duty. How... inconvenient for you both."

"What's that supposed to mean?" Eden demanded, though she could feel through her connection to Kade that he already knew and was dreading the answer.

"It means that eliminating one of you will cause the other considerable suffering," Ravencrest replied with clinical interest. "Guardian bonds aren't just magical connections—they're emotional entanglements that make rational decision-making almost impossible. Your predecessor understood this, which is why she eventually chose isolation over risk of compromise through personal attachment."

Eden felt ice form in her veins as she understood tactical implications. Any threat to Kade would force her to choose between her mission and his safety, while any threat to her would make him vulnerable to the kind of emotional manipulation that could turn a protector into a liability.

But underneath the strategic concern was something else—fury so pure it made her vision white at edges. This man was threatening the person who'd awakened her abilities, shown her what she could become, chosen to stand with her against the entire magical establishment.

"But perhaps a demonstration would be more instructive than explanation," Ravencrest continued, raising his hand toward Kade with casual certainty that his authority was absolute.

What happened next occurred so quickly that Eden's enhanced perception barely had time to process sequence of events.

Ravencrest's attack—something that looked like winter given malevolent form—struck Kade with force designed not to kill but to cause the kind of exquisite agony that would force Eden to surrender rather than watch him suffer.

Eden's response was immediate and overwhelming—not controlled magic she'd been learning to use, but something that erupted from deepest parts of her consciousness like molten gold given violent form. The hotel suite exploded around them as reality bent to accommodate power that transcended anything individual consciousness should have been able to channel.

But it was what came after the explosion of force that proved most significant.

Instead of chaos that Ravencrest had expected, Eden's power began to stabilize in patterns suggesting she was drawing strength from sources he couldn't perceive or counter. Through her connections to Underground network, through her bonds with practitioners who'd committed themselves to her cause, through something that felt like conscious approval of reality itself—power flowed into her with surgical precision.

And more than that, she was drawing on knowledge she'd absorbed from Cordelia. The Collector's techniques for consciousness manipulation, for reality shaping, for exerting control over other practitioners—all of it was available to her now, refined by her own growing understanding of how power worked.

"Impossible," Ravencrest breathed, his attack dissolving as he realized that his centuries of accumulated knowledge had just encountered something that operated according to completely different principles. "No individual practitioner should be able to channel cooperative power on that scale—"

"I'm not just an individual practitioner," Eden replied, her power now blazing around her like a second sun. "I'm part of something larger, something that exists because people chose to support it rather than because they were forced to submit to it."

She gestured, and power she was channeling focused on Ravencrest with surgical precision. Not seeking to destroy or control, but to demonstrate difference between authority based on fear and leadership based on voluntary alliance.

But more than that, she was trying to consume him. Using techniques absorbed from Cordelia, she reached out with abilities designed to drain his knowledge, his experience, his accumulated power. She wanted everything he knew about the Council's operations, their resources, their plans.

The effect was immediate and instructive. Ravencrest's carefully maintained composure cracked as he felt what it was like to be on receiving end of power that transcended individual ambition or institutional authority. For the first time in centuries, he was experiencing magic that operated according to principles of consumption rather than simple domination.

"What are you doing?" he demanded, backing away as Eden's influence began to work its way through psychological defenses that had been constructed over centuries of careful predation.

"Learning everything you know about the Council's operations," Eden replied, her voice carrying harmonics that seemed to resonate across impossible distances. "Absorbing your knowledge, your experience, your understanding of how magical authority really works."

For a moment, she felt his memories flowing into her consciousness—decades of enforcement actions, systematic elimination of threats, the Council's true purpose and methods. It was intoxicating, like drinking wine made from distilled power and knowledge.

But then something pushed back. Ravencrest's will, refined by centuries of maintaining control over others, proved stronger than she'd expected. He managed to break her attempt at consumption, though she could see the effort cost him considerably.

"Fascinating," he said, though his voice carried less conviction than at confrontation's beginning. "You've learned to combine voluntary alliance with forced extraction. That's... novel."

"What you represent is ending," Eden said, her voice carrying harmonics that seemed to resonate across impossible distances. "Not because I'm destroying it, but because people are choosing something better."

"This is rebellion," Ravencrest said, though his voice carried less conviction than when he'd arrived. "This is chaos, breakdown of everything that's kept magical society stable for centuries—"

"This is evolution," Eden replied, her power now encompassing not just herself but everyone who'd chosen to stand with her against Council's version of order. "This is what happens when people stop accepting limitations imposed by those who profit from their compliance."

Around them, transformed hotel was beginning to resonate with energies suggesting confrontation was affecting magical practitioners throughout Salem, throughout New England, perhaps throughout entire continent. Underground network was activating, independent practitioners were making choices about which side they wanted to support, and even some Council loyalists were beginning to question whether their organization's methods were worth costs they imposed on everyone else.

The sensation of power flowing toward her from dozens of sources made Eden's hunger roar with satisfaction. This was what she'd been craving—not just individual magical ability, but influence that could reshape entire systems of authority.

"You killed my mother," Eden continued, her voice taking on new harmonics that made Ravencrest actually step backward. "You've killed dozens of others who refused to submit to your authority. You've turned magical practice into a system of oppression disguised as order."

"All necessary measures—"

"All choices made by people who confused their desire for control with needs of community they claimed to serve." Eden's smile was beautiful and terrible and utterly without mercy. "But here's what you never understood, Magistrate—authority without consent is just organized violence, and violence eventually faces something stronger than itself."

She raised her hands, and Ravencrest felt something he hadn't experienced in centuries—genuine fear. Not of death or defeat, but of irrelevance, of discovering that power structure he'd spent his life maintaining was nothing more than elaborate illusion supported by careful propaganda and strategic intimidation.

The craving in her chest focused on him with laser intensity. She needed his knowledge, his understanding of Council operations, his accumulated experience with magical politics. But more than that, she needed to consume him completely, to add his power to her own growing arsenal.

"The Council will not tolerate this disruption," he said, but he was already beginning to fade, retreating to whatever stronghold his organization maintained for situations where direct confrontation proved inadvisable. "There will be consequences for this defiance extending far beyond what you can imagine."

"Let me save you some time," Eden replied, her voice carrying enough power to make reality itself seem to bend around her words. "The consequences are that magical society is going to be free to develop according to its own nature rather than your organization's paranoia. Practitioners are going to cooperate because it serves their interests, not because they're forced to submit to institutional authority. And people like you are going to discover what it feels like to be irrelevant."

As High Magistrate disappeared and immediate threat receded, Eden found herself standing in a hotel suite transformed into something existing partially outside normal space-time, surrounded by allies whose commitment to change had proven stronger than Council's commitment to maintaining control.

But the victory felt different from her previous confrontations. This time, she hadn't just defended herself or liberated others—she'd proven that cooperation could match institutional authority when stakes were high enough, and she'd successfully absorbed knowledge and techniques from multiple powerful practitioners.

The hunger that had been consuming her since her awakening was evolving again, becoming something more sophisticated and demanding. She didn't just want power anymore—she wanted everything. Every technique, every secret, every practitioner who could serve her purposes or be consumed for their knowledge.

"What happens now?" Kade asked, though his tone suggested he already suspected the answer.

"Now we stop pretending this is about individual conflicts and acknowledge that we're fighting a war," Eden replied, her eyes blazing with golden light that seemed to carry its own gravity. "Ravencrest's made their position clear—they'd rather eliminate everyone who disagrees with them than risk any change to system that gives them power."

She looked out through windows that now showed not just Salem but magical communities throughout North America, all processing what they'd witnessed, all making choices about what kind of world they wanted to live in.

The craving in her chest had evolved into something that demanded satisfaction on a scale she'd never imagined. She wanted to consume the entire magical establishment, to reshape it according to her vision, to become something so powerful that no one would ever dare to threaten her or those she chose to protect again.

"The revolution isn't coming anymore," she said, her voice carrying harmonics that seemed to resonate across impossible distances. "The revolution is here. And we're going to win it."

But even as she spoke, Eden could feel something else building in spaces between dimensions—not just Council resistance, but recognition from forces that operated on scales far beyond human politics. Her confrontation with Ravencrest had attracted attention from consciousness structures that viewed magical society as just one small part of much larger patterns.

The real test was just beginning. And Eden Morrow was discovering that her appetite for power might have no upper limit at all.

CHAPTER FIFTEEN

The Underground Network

The message arrived hidden in a bouquet of black roses that bloomed only at midnight, their petals releasing jasmine and secrets when Eden touched them.

She found them on her windowsill, arranged with careful artistry that spoke of someone who understood the language of flowers and power. Tucked among the stems was a scroll written in silver ink that moved across parchment like living mercury:

The ravens gather at the crossroads when the moon is dark. Those who seek alternatives to the Council's authority are always welcome at our table. Come alone if you dare.

Recognition phrase: "The shadows have eyes." Response phrase: "But the darkness offers freedom."

No signature, but the magical resonance made Eden's senses tingle with recognition of something operating in the spaces between official authority and complete chaos. The hunger that had been growing since her encounter with Ravencrest sharpened into curious anticipation—here was another source of knowledge, another network to potentially claim and consume.

"The Underground," Kade said when she showed him the message, his silver eyes thoughtful. "I'd heard whispers, but I wasn't certain they existed."

"What kind of whispers?"

"Stories about practitioners who've gone completely off the grid—invisible to Council tracking, helping others escape magical bonds, political alliances, arranged marriages between houses." He set the scroll down carefully, as if it might explode. "People who've learned to operate outside every established framework."

Eden felt possibility race through her enhanced awareness, but underneath the excitement was something more predatory. These people had knowledge she needed, techniques she craved, resources she could absorb and make her own.

"They sound like my kind of people."

"They also sound dangerous. Operating that far outside normal magical society... there's no telling what compromises they've made to stay invisible."

"Only one way to find out." She was already planning preparations for the evening, anticipation making her skin flush with heat. "The crossroads— do you know where that might be?"

Kade nodded reluctantly. "Ten miles north. Where a colonial coach road intersects with what used to be a Native trading path. It's been neutral ground for centuries."

That evening, Eden drove through countryside that grew progressively wilder as she left Ravenshollow's influence. Roads narrowed to gravel, then deer paths, while trees pressed closer until their branches blocked most starlight. She didn't need directions—something in her enhanced awareness was drawn to the crossroads like a compass seeking true north, like a predator following the scent of prey.

The hunger in her chest intensified with each mile. She was about to meet others who understood what it meant to crave freedom, to need power, to be willing to sacrifice everything for the chance to become something extraordinary. But more than that, she was about to encounter practitioners who'd developed techniques outside Council oversight—methods she could study, absorb, improve upon.

She found it beneath a centuries-old oak, the ground worn smooth by countless meetings. The air itself seemed thick with accumulated magic from decades of clandestine rituals, and Eden could taste the residue of power that had been wielded here by those who refused to accept the limitations others tried to impose on them.

At precisely midnight, they began to appear—not dramatically, but with subtle skill that spoke of years perfecting the art of not being noticed. They stepped from shadows that had seemed empty, materialized from behind inadequate trees, emerged from solid ground as if the earth itself had concealed them.

Perhaps a dozen practitioners, various ages and backgrounds, all sharing the watchful wariness that marked people who'd learned to survive in hostile territory. They dressed practically, in clothes that wouldn't attract mundane attention but that Eden's senses detected were warded with sophisticated protective enchantments.

The woman who approached first appeared to be in her forties, graying brown hair in a practical ponytail, clothes suggesting physical labor. But her eyes held depths of knowledge and carefully contained fury, and when she smiled, Eden caught glimpses of power that made her own abilities sing in recognition—and hunger.

"Lady Morrow," she said, her voice carrying a faint accent that might have been Irish or something far older. "Thank you for accepting our invitation.

I'm Moira, and these are my associates in enterprises the Council prefers didn't exist."

Moira's weathered hands bore scars that told stories—burn marks from a Council "questioning" twenty years ago, when she'd refused to reveal safe house locations. She'd lost her sister that night, watched Elena dissolve into nothing because Moira chose protecting strangers over family. Every practitioner she helped escape was Elena's ghost, demanding she choose better this time.

The pain in the woman's memories made Eden's hunger spike with sympathetic resonance, but underneath the empathy was something more calculating. This woman had survived Council interrogation, had maintained her secrets under extreme duress. That kind of mental discipline was exactly what Eden needed to learn.

"Such as?" Eden asked, noting how the others had arranged themselves in a loose circle that managed to be both welcoming and defensible.

"Survival, primarily," replied a tall man with silver-streaked hair and scars suggesting extensive experience with violence. "Helping others survive. Preserving knowledge certain authorities prefer buried."

Marcus traced the scar along his jaw—souvenir from the Vancouver Incident, when he'd led a Council strike team against hedge witch families. The father had gotten off one spell before Marcus cut him down: a curse that let Marcus feel every death he'd caused. Forty-seven souls whispered his name in darkness. Following Eden was his only chance at balance, his only hope of finding redemption through service to someone who might actually deserve his loyalty.

The weight of his guilt and desperate hope made Eden's craving intensify, but she was also cataloging his skills. Military training, tactical expertise, knowledge of Council operations—all potentially valuable resources she could claim through alliance or other means.

"We heard about your difficulties with Council representatives," added a younger woman whose punk aesthetic couldn't hide the power radiating from her like forge heat. "Word travels fast when someone tells Seraphina Blackthorne where she can stick her cooperation offers."

Luna's punk appearance hid MIT degrees in computer science and theoretical physics. The Council had recruited her at sixteen—youngest ever admitted to their research division. She'd spent three years perfecting surveillance spells that hunted her own people before her conscience cracked. The blood on her hands was digital, but it still counted. Every algorithm she'd written had led to someone's capture, someone's death.

The technical knowledge locked in Luna's mind made Eden's mouth water with anticipation. Here was expertise she desperately needed—understanding of how modern technology interfaced with magical practice, knowledge of Council surveillance methods, skills that could be adapted to serve her own purposes.

Eden felt satisfaction at the reminder of her confrontation with Seraphina. "I defended my home and the people I care about."

"Nothing more?" Moira's laugh was rich, carrying appreciation and hope. "Dear one, you accomplished something that hasn't happened in two centuries—you faced down one of the Council's most dangerous operatives and sent her running without killing anyone. That takes power and restraint in equal measure."

"What kind of restraint?"

"The kind that comes from thinking about consequences rather than immediate gratification," Marcus said, stepping forward with obvious respect. "The kind that suggests you understand the difference between winning battles and winning wars."

His voice carried military precision haunted by past violence, seeing everything through tactical lenses that weighed acceptable losses against strategic gains. Eden could feel his expertise calling to her, knowledge she desperately wanted to possess and make her own.

Eden felt her interest sharpen. These people understood conflict, strategy, the difference between random rebellion and organized resistance. They had skills she needed, experience she craved, resources she could absorb and improve upon.

"And you think I might be interested in winning a war?"

"We think you might want alternatives to the current power structure," Moira replied carefully. "Ways of practicing magic that don't require Council registration, submission to their politics, or acceptance of arbitrary limitations on what knowledge can be shared."

"At what cost?"

"Isolation from mainstream magical society," Luna said bluntly, her street vernacular mixing with technical precision. "Constant vigilance against discovery. Complete self-sufficiency in ways most practitioners never consider."

"But also freedom," added another voice—an older man whose expensive clothes couldn't hide the predatory awareness that marked him as someone who'd survived by being more dangerous than his enemies. "Freedom to develop abilities according to your own judgment. Freedom to help others do the same. Freedom to imagine magical practices the Council never dreamed of."

Eden walked slowly around the circle, studying faces and letting her enhanced senses evaluate the magical signatures of each person present.

What she found was remarkable—not desperate refugees or fanatics, but experienced, capable people who'd made deliberate choices about how to live their lives.

The hunger in her chest roared with approval. These weren't just potential allies—they were resources, sources of knowledge and power she could absorb and use to further her own growth. Each person represented decades of experience, specialized skills, understanding of magical society's hidden operations.

"How many of you are there?"

"More than the Council suspects, fewer than we need," Moira replied diplomatically. "We don't think of ourselves as a single organization—that would make us too easy to track. Instead, we're a network of individuals and small groups sharing values, occasionally coordinating for mutual benefit."

"What kind of coordination?"

"Information sharing," Marcus said. "Early warning about enforcement actions. Safe houses for people needing to disappear quickly. Resources for developing abilities outside approved categories."

"And sometimes," Luna added with a grin that was all teeth and mischief, "more direct action against those who abuse their authority."

Eden felt the familiar thrill of possibility mixing with warranted caution. What these people described sounded exactly like what she needed—allies who understood that the Council's system was broken, resources for unrestricted development, proof that she wasn't alone in believing that change was necessary and possible.

But more than that, they represented opportunities. Knowledge to be gained, skills to be learned, power to be claimed through association and, if necessary, consumption. Each person here had something she wanted, and she was beginning to understand that want and need were becoming indistinguishable from her right to possess.

"What do you want from me?"

"What we've always wanted," Moira said simply. "Freedom to practice according to conscience and ability. Protection for those who can't protect themselves. An end to the Council's monopoly on legitimate magical authority."

"And you think I can provide those things?"

"We think you're the first person in centuries with both the power and the position to effectively challenge the status quo," the older man said, his dark eyes gleaming with anticipation. "The question is whether you're willing to try."

Eden looked around the circle one more time, seeing not just individual faces but representation of a movement that had been building in shadows for decades. These people had been waiting for someone like her—someone with enough power to stand against the Council, enough legitimacy to attract allies, enough vision to imagine something better.

The craving that had been consuming her since her awakening suddenly found perfect focus. She didn't just want power anymore—she wanted everything these people could offer her, and everything she could take from them once she'd proven her superiority. They would serve her willingly or unwillingly, but they would serve.

"I'll need more information," she said finally. "About your network, your resources, your long-term goals. About the specific threats we'd face and the support I could expect."

"Of course," Moira agreed. "But first, we need to know whether you're genuinely interested in joining our cause or simply gathering intelligence for your own purposes."

Eden took a deep breath, feeling the weight of decision settling on her shoulders. But underneath the responsibility was anticipation, hunger, the growing certainty that these people represented exactly what she needed to feed the cravings that were consuming her.

"I'm interested. More than interested. The Council's made clear they see me as a threat to contain or eliminate. I'd rather work with people who see me as an ally to support—and to learn from."

The response was immediate and enthusiastic—not just from the speakers, but from every member of the group. Eden could feel their excitement, their hope, their growing belief that change might actually be possible.

But more than that, she could feel their power, their knowledge, their accumulated experiences. All of it within her reach now, ready to be claimed through alliance, manipulation, or whatever other methods proved necessary. They thought they were recruiting her, but Eden was beginning to understand that the relationship would flow in quite the opposite direction.

"Then welcome to the Underground, Lady Morrow," Marcus said with a grin that transformed his harsh features. "Things are about to get very interesting."

As the group dispersed, each providing different contact methods and information about coordination meetings, Eden felt the familiar sensation of her world expanding to accommodate new possibilities. But this time, instead of simply reacting to circumstances beyond her control, she was actively choosing her path forward.

The Council had declared war by sending Seraphina, the dream walker, and Ravencrest. Now it was time to build the alliance that would let her fight back on her own terms—and satisfy the hunger that demanded she become something far greater than what she had been.

The game was changing, the stakes were rising, and Eden Morrow was no longer playing defense. She was learning to hunt, to claim, to consume everything the magical world had to offer.

But as she drove back through the darkened countryside toward Ravenshollow, Eden felt something else stirring in her consciousness—knowledge absorbed from Cordelia, techniques learned from observing Council methods, understanding of how consciousness could be shaped and controlled. The Underground thought they were gaining a powerful ally, but Eden was beginning to realize they might have found something else entirely.

The craving that had brought her to that crossroads was only the beginning of appetites she was just starting to understand. And she was discovering that her hunger might have no natural limits at all.

CHAPTER SIXTEEN

The War Council

Within a week of her meeting with the Underground, Eden's world had transformed from a sanctuary of magical learning into the nerve center of what could only be described as a revolution in the making.

Ravenshollow's rooms rearranged themselves to accommodate the steady stream of visitors who arrived under cover of darkness—practitioners whose existence the official magical world preferred to ignore, refugees from the Council's increasingly aggressive enforcement actions, and rebels whose only crime had been believing that magical power should serve growth rather than control.

Eden stood in what had once been the manor's secondary library, now transformed into a war room that would have impressed any military strategist. Maps covered every available surface, showing not just the geographical distribution of Underground safe houses and Council strongholds, but the complex networks of alliance and enmity that defined magical politics throughout North America.

The hunger that had been consuming her since her awakening had evolved into something more sophisticated—she craved not just power, but influence, control, the ability to reshape the magical world according to her vision. Each new ally was another resource to be claimed, another source of knowledge to be absorbed, another step toward the dominion she was beginning to understand she'd always been meant to claim.

"The pattern is becoming clear," said Dr. Sarah Chen, a former Council researcher who had fled their organization after discovering some particularly disturbing experiments they had been conducting on captured practitioners. She was a small, precise woman in her fifties whose unassuming appearance concealed one of the most brilliant strategic minds Eden had ever encountered. "They're not just trying to contain individual threats anymore—they're implementing a systematic campaign to eliminate independent magical practice entirely."

Dr. Sarah Chen's scientific precision hid emotional trauma and maternal protectiveness earned through twenty years in the Council research division. She'd joined believing they were preventing another Salem, only to discover experiments on "volunteers"—memory extraction, consciousness transfer, forced bloodline evolution. She'd told herself it served the greater good until she saw what they did to children. Magical genetics. They weren't just studying power—they were breeding it.

The knowledge locked in Dr. Chen's mind made Eden's mouth water with anticipation. Here was someone who understood the Council's deepest secrets, their most classified research, their methods for manipulating magical bloodlines. All of it potentially hers to claim and use.

"Meaning?" Eden asked, though she suspected the answer would be both illuminating and infuriating.

"Meaning they've decided that the safest way to maintain their authority is to ensure that no one else has enough power to challenge it," replied Marcus Webb, the scarred man from the crossroads meeting whose full background Eden was still learning to appreciate. "Registration isn't about oversight anymore—it's about identification, cataloging potential threats so they can be eliminated before they become problematic."

Eden felt her power stir in response to the casual way he described such systematic oppression, golden light beginning to flicker behind her eyes.

Around the room, maps began to glow with their own inner radiance as her magic responded to her emotional state, highlighting Council positions in hostile red while Underground safe houses blazed with welcoming gold.

The display made her hunger spike with satisfaction. This was what power should look like—reality itself bending to accommodate her will, responding to her emotional state, serving her purposes. But more than that, she was beginning to understand that the same techniques could be applied to people as well as objects.

"How many independents have they eliminated in the past year?" she asked, though part of her wasn't sure she wanted to know the answer.

"Forty-seven confirmed," Luna Martinez replied from her position at the communication array she had set up in one corner of the room. The young woman with the punk rock aesthetic had proven remarkably skilled at both magical reconnaissance and electronic surveillance, creating information networks that put conventional intelligence agencies to shame. "Another dozen possibles where the deaths could have been natural but the timing was suspiciously convenient."

"Forty-seven," Eden repeated, letting the number sink into her consciousness. "Forty-seven practitioners killed simply for refusing to submit to Council authority."

"And that's just the ones we know about," Dr. Chen added grimly. "The Council has become very good at making deaths look accidental, or at eliminating people so completely that they simply... disappear from all records."

Eden moved to the largest map, which showed the entire North American continent marked with pins that tracked the shifting allegiances of major magical communities. Red pins indicated confirmed Council loyalists, blue showed Underground allies, and yellow marked practitioners whose positions remained uncertain or unknown.

There were far too many red pins for her comfort, and not nearly enough blue ones. But more than that, she could see the patterns now—the way power flowed through the magical community, the key individuals whose allegiances could shift entire regions, the chokepoints where decisive action could reshape the entire conflict.

The craving in her chest sharpened into predatory focus. She needed those key individuals, needed to claim their loyalty or eliminate their opposition. But more than that, she was beginning to understand that loyalty based on fear and dependency was far more reliable than loyalty based on principle or affection.

"We need to change the equation," she said, her enhanced vision noting patterns and connections that weren't immediately obvious to normal perception. "Right now, we're playing their game by their rules—hiding, reacting, trying to survive their systematic elimination of independent practitioners. That's not sustainable."

"What are you suggesting?" Marcus asked, though his tone suggested he already suspected the direction of her thoughts.

"I'm suggesting we stop hiding." Eden turned to face the assembled group, her eyes blazing with golden light that made the war room's magical implements hum with sympathetic vibrations. "I'm suggesting we make it impossible for magical society to ignore what's happening, force practitioners to choose sides instead of pretending they can remain neutral while the Council systematically destroys everyone who threatens their monopoly."

The hunger in her chest roared with approval. This was what she'd been craving without knowing it—not just power, but the chance to use that power on a scale that would reshape everything. She wanted to remake the magical world, to claim dominion over every practitioner who might serve her purposes.

"That's..." Dr. Chen paused, clearly working through the implications. "That's essentially declaring open war against the most powerful magical authority in North America."

"They declared war on us first," Luna pointed out with characteristic bluntness. "The question is whether we're going to keep pretending this is about individual conflicts instead of systematic oppression."

"What did you have in mind?" asked a new voice from the doorway. Eden turned to see Moira entering the war room, followed by three other Underground operatives whose arrival suggested important developments in their intelligence gathering.

"A demonstration," Eden replied, the idea crystallizing as she spoke. "Something public, undeniable, impossible to dismiss as the actions of isolated malcontents. Something that forces every practitioner in North America to acknowledge what the Council really represents."

The craving in her chest focused into laser intensity. This was what she needed—a stage large enough to display her power, an audience significant enough to make her dominance meaningful, an opportunity to claim not just victory but complete authority over the magical world.

"What kind of demonstration?" Moira asked, though her expression suggested both intrigue and concern in equal measure.

"The kind that shows them what we're capable of when we're not constrained by their arbitrary limitations," Eden said, her smile sharp and beautiful and utterly confident. "The kind that proves alternatives to their authority aren't just possible, but superior."

She moved to a section of the map that showed the Eastern Seaboard, her finger tracing a route that connected several major magical communities. "There's a gathering next month—the Autumn Convergence in Salem. Every significant magical family, organization, and independent practitioner on the East Coast will be there. Representatives from European magical communities, observers from the Pacific Coast councils, even some of the more reclusive solitary practitioners who rarely leave their territories."

"You want to recruit them," Marcus said, understanding immediately where her thoughts were leading.

"I want to offer them a choice," Eden corrected, though the distinction was becoming blurred in her mind. She didn't just want to offer choices—she wanted to shape them, control them, ensure that the only reasonable option was to submit to her vision of what the magical world should become. "Between the status quo and something better. Between serving a system that sees them as resources to be exploited and joining a movement that recognizes their inherent worth and potential."

But even as she spoke, Eden was thinking about the techniques she'd absorbed from Cordelia, the methods for consciousness manipulation she'd been studying and refining. The practitioners at Salem wouldn't just be choosing freely—they would be choosing under the influence of power they couldn't recognize or resist.

"The risks would be enormous," Dr. Chen pointed out with academic precision. "The Council would interpret any public recruitment effort as an act of war. They'd respond with everything they have."

"Let them respond," Eden replied, her voice taking on harmonics that made the very air tremble with contained power. "I'm tired of tiptoeing around their sensibilities while they systematically murder anyone who disagrees with their policies. It's time to find out how many practitioners are ready to stand up and say 'enough.'"

The silence that followed was charged with possibility and danger in equal measure. What Eden was proposing would fundamentally alter the balance of power in magical society, forcing conflicts that had been simmering beneath the surface for decades into open confrontation.

It was also, Eden realized as she looked around the room at faces that showed both excitement and terror, exactly what needed to happen. The hunger that had been consuming her since her awakening had evolved into something far more ambitious than personal power—she wanted to remake the entire magical world, to claim dominion over every practitioner who might serve her purposes.

And she was beginning to understand that she had the tools to make that vision reality.

"The Salem Convergence is neutral ground," Moira said slowly, clearly working through the practical implications. "Ancient treaties, binding oaths, magical protections that make violence on the gathering grounds virtually impossible."

"Which makes it the perfect place to make a statement without worrying about immediate retaliation," Luna added with growing enthusiasm. "Whatever we do there, they'd have to respond afterward, on ground of our choosing."

"What kind of statement?" Marcus asked, his tactical mind already evaluating scenarios and contingencies.

Eden felt the familiar thrill of a plan coming together, pieces falling into place with the satisfying click of tumblers in a lock. The craving in her chest focused into laser intensity—she needed this victory, needed to prove her dominance on a scale that would satisfy the hunger consuming her.

"The kind that demonstrates what magical practice could look like without the Council's restrictions. Public displays of techniques they claim are too dangerous to teach, collaborative magic that shows what practitioners can accomplish when they're not competing for limited resources, innovations that prove their 'traditional methods' are holding everyone back."

"And if they try to stop us?" Dr. Chen asked.

"Then we prove that their authority depends on consent rather than inherent legitimacy," Eden replied, her power now blazing around her like a second sun. "And that consent can be withdrawn."

But what she didn't say was that she was also planning to prove something else—that consent could be manufactured, shaped, directed through techniques that made resistance not just difficult but literally unthinkable. The practitioners at Salem would choose to follow her, and they would believe that choice was entirely their own.

As the planning session continued deep into the night, Eden felt the familiar sensation of standing at the edge of something transformative. But this time, instead of simply accepting change as it happened to her, she was actively creating the conditions for the kind of transformation she wanted to see in the world.

The Council had spent centuries maintaining their authority through fear, manipulation, and the systematic elimination of alternatives. It was time to show the magical world that their supposed monopoly on legitimate power was nothing more than an elaborate lie supported by careful propaganda and strategic violence.

But more than that, it was time to demonstrate what real authority looked like—not the crude domination the Council practiced, but the elegant control she was learning to wield. Power that made its subjects grateful for their submission, that convinced them they were choosing freely even as their choices were shaped by forces they couldn't perceive.

The hunger that had brought her to Ravenshollow was evolving into something far grander—the need to consume not just power, but entire systems of authority. She would reshape the magical world according to her vision, and everyone would have to choose whether to serve her willingly or discover what happened to those who proved themselves unnecessary.

The revolution was no longer a distant possibility—it was an immediate necessity. And Eden Morrow was ready to lead it, to feed the cravings that demanded she become something far greater than any single practitioner had ever been.

The question was no longer whether she would succeed, but how much of the magical world would recognize her authority when she was finished claiming it.

The Declaration

The broadcast reached every magical practitioner in North America simultaneously—not through any technology the mundane world would recognize, but through techniques that had been theoretical until Eden's enhanced abilities made them practical reality.

She stood in Ravenshollow's great hall, which had transformed itself for the occasion into something existing partially in normal space and partially in dimensions where communication transcended physical limitations. Around her, representatives of the Underground network, former Council operatives who'd chosen to defect, and independent practitioners who'd committed themselves to change created a visual demonstration of the alliance she was announcing to the world.

But more than that, she was drawing power from each of them—not obviously, not in ways they would notice, but with techniques refined from her study of Cordelia's methods. Their emotional investment in her words, their hope for change, their desperate need for leadership—all of it fed the hunger that had been consuming her since her awakening.

"My name is Eden Morrow," she began, her voice carrying across impossible distances to reach practitioners in hidden sanctuaries, urban covens, academic institutions, and corporate boardrooms throughout the continent. "Six months ago, I was living a mundane life in New York City, completely unaware that magic existed or that I carried one of the most powerful magical bloodlines in North American history."

The response was immediate—not audible through the broadcast medium, but perceptible through magical resonances connecting every practitioner listening. Surprise, curiosity, skepticism, and in some cases, recognition of power that made even the most jaded observers pay attention.

Eden felt each response like a physical touch, and she was hungry for more. She needed their attention, their emotional investment, their growing conviction that she represented something they'd been waiting for without knowing it.

"Today, I stand before you as someone who's experienced both the wonder of awakening to magical potential and the horror of discovering what certain authorities will do to maintain their monopoly on that power."

She paused, letting the words sink in while she subtly drew more energy from her audience. Through the mystical communication network, she could feel thousands of practitioners' attention focused on her with almost physical intensity, and she fed on it like wine.

"I've been attacked by Council enforcers who prefer elimination to education. I've faced collectors who see practitioners as objects to be acquired rather than people to be respected. I've confronted authorities who believe that power gives them the right to make choices for everyone else, regardless of consent or consequence."

Through her enhanced awareness, Eden could sense the moment when her words began to resonate with listeners who'd spent years or decades believing exactly what she was contradicting. But more than that, she was using techniques absorbed from Cordelia to subtly influence their emotional responses, making her words seem more compelling, her cause more just, her authority more natural and inevitable.

"But I've also discovered something that the Council doesn't want you to know," she continued, her voice growing stronger as she approached her message's heart. "You don't have to choose between submission and elimination. You don't have to accept that compliance with their authority or complete isolation from magical society are your only options."

The response was building like a storm on the horizon—not just from the Underground network, but from practitioners throughout North America who'd been waiting for exactly this kind of alternative. Eden could feel their hunger for change, their desperate need for leadership, their growing certainty that she represented something they'd been craving without knowing it.

And she fed on all of it, drawing strength and satisfaction from thousands of practitioners' emotional investment in her vision.

"There is a third option," she said, and power flowed through her voice with such intensity that several listeners later reported reality itself seemed to shift around them as they heard the words. "The voluntary choice to work together because we share common values and goals, not because we're forced to submit to someone else's definition of order."

"Today, we formally announce the creation of the Covenant of Free Practitioners—a voluntary association dedicated to supporting magical development according to individual conscience and capability, protecting those who cannot protect themselves, and ensuring that no practitioner is ever again forced to choose between freedom and survival."

The response was immediate and overwhelming—not just from the Underground network, but from practitioners throughout North America who'd been waiting for exactly this kind of alternative. Magical signatures blazed to life in cities and wilderness areas, academic institutions and private residences, as hundreds of people made the instantaneous decision to publicly declare their support for change.

But Eden could feel something else happening—through the mystical communication network, she was establishing connections to each practitioner who responded positively to her message. Subtle links that would allow her to influence them later, to shape their thoughts and choices, to ensure their loyalty went deeper than mere intellectual agreement.

"This is rebellion," came a voice that Eden recognized as belonging to Magistrate Blackthorne, cutting through the communication network with authority that made several listeners physically recoil. "This is the breakdown of everything that's kept magical society stable and secure for three centuries."

"You think me a tyrant?" Seraphina's presence blazed through the mystical network like winter given form. "I was there during the Cascade Wars, child. I watched Seattle melt into glass when untrained practitioners tried to 'cooperate' on workings they didn't understand. I held dying children whose parents thought freedom mattered more than wisdom. Your revolution isn't noble—it's history's most violent mistake preparing to repeat itself."

"I offer choice," Eden replied calmly, her power easily matching the Magistrate's attempt to dominate the broadcast. "The same choice that should be available to every conscious being—the right to determine their own path, make their own mistakes, and accept responsibility for their own decisions."

But even as she spoke of choice, Eden was using techniques learned from studying Cordelia's methods to subtly influence every practitioner listening. Their emotional responses, their growing certainty that she was right, their increasing conviction that following her was not just reasonable but necessary—all of it was being shaped by power they couldn't recognize or resist.

"And when those decisions lead to catastrophe? When unguided practitioners cause the magical disasters that necessitated the Council's creation?"

Eden's smile was radiant and terrible and utterly without compromise. "Then we'll deal with the consequences together, as allies working toward common solutions, rather than as subjects hoping their rulers will protect them from dangers they're not allowed to understand."

The confrontation that followed played out across the entire North American magical community—not physical violence, but a battle of ideas, philosophies, and fundamental assumptions about the nature of power and authority. Through the mystical communication network, every practitioner on the continent became witness to the conflict that would determine magical society's future.

But Eden had learned something from her previous encounters with Council authority. This wasn't about winning arguments or demonstrating superior force. This was about offering people something they'd never had before—the illusion of genuine choice while ensuring they made the choices she needed them to make.

"Join us," she said, addressing not just those already sympathetic to her cause but everyone who'd ever felt constrained by systems they had no voice in creating. "Not because you must, but because you choose to. Not because you're afraid of the consequences of refusal, but because you believe in the possibility of something better."

Through the mystical network, she began to share something that couldn't be conveyed through words alone—but it wasn't just the experience of magical practice freed from institutional limitations. It was a carefully crafted sensation designed to create dependency, to make practitioners feel that they needed her guidance, her protection, her continued presence in their lives.

The effect was subtle but profound. Every practitioner who opened themselves to her influence found themselves convinced that Eden Morrow wasn't just offering an alternative to Council authority—she was offering salvation itself.

"This is what cooperation feels like," she said, her voice carrying harmonics that seemed to resonate in dimensions most listeners couldn't perceive. "This is what magic becomes when it serves growth rather than control."

The silence that followed was profound, charged with the understanding that they'd experienced something that would reshape their conception of what magical society could become. But more than that, hundreds of practitioners now carried within them a need they couldn't name—a conviction that their wellbeing, their magical development, their very survival depended on maintaining their connection to Eden Morrow.

Then came voices from across the continent—not arguments or challenges, but questions. Hundreds of them, from practitioners who'd never dared to imagine alternatives to the Council's authority suddenly wondering what might be possible if they were free to find out.

But Eden could hear something else in their voices—dependency, need, the growing conviction that she alone could provide the guidance and protection they desperately craved.

"How do we begin?" asked someone from the Pacific Northwest.

"What happens to those who choose differently?" came a voice from the Great Lakes region.

"How do we protect ourselves without becoming what we're fighting against?" asked a practitioner from the Deep South.

Eden felt her heart expand as she realized what was happening. This wasn't just recruitment or political organizing—this was the birth of something genuinely new, a form of magical society based on what appeared to be voluntary association but was actually sophisticated psychological control.

"We begin by choosing," she said, her voice carrying enough power to make reality itself seem more malleable, more responsive to individual will. "We begin by taking responsibility for our own development while accepting the guidance of those who've walked this path before us. We begin by proving that cooperation is more powerful than coercion, that alliance is stronger than authority, that people working together under proper leadership can achieve things that no individual or institution ever could."

As the broadcast ended and the mystical communication network dissolved back into potential, Eden found herself surrounded by allies whose expressions showed everything from exhilaration to terror at the magnitude of what they'd accomplished.

But more than that, she could feel the connections she'd established—hundreds of threads linking her consciousness to practitioners across the continent, each one a potential source of power, knowledge, and absolute loyalty.

"Response?" she asked, though she could already feel the answer building like a storm on the horizon of her enhanced awareness.

"Unprecedented," Dr. Chen replied, her voice tight with amazement and concern. "We're receiving formal alliance requests from practitioners and organizations throughout the continent. But we're also seeing Council enforcement teams mobilizing on a scale that suggests they're preparing for all-out war."

"Let them prepare," Eden said, her eyes blazing with golden light that seemed to carry its own gravity. "We've just offered every practitioner in North America the choice between freedom and tyranny. Now we find out how many of them are wise enough to make the right choice."

But even as she spoke, Eden could feel something else building through the connections that now linked her to practitioners across the continent—not just support or opposition, but a third response she hadn't anticipated.

Worship. Devotion. The growing realization among thousands of people that they'd never really understood what they were capable of because they'd never been fortunate enough to have proper guidance.

The revolution was no longer theoretical. It was becoming reality, one carefully manipulated choice at a time.

And Eden Morrow was ready to help guide it into whatever form would best serve her ever-growing appetite for power and control.

The hunger that had brought her to Ravenshollow was evolving into something far more sophisticated and demanding. She didn't just want magical authority anymore—she wanted conscious beings who would serve her willingly, gratefully, believing that their submission was the greatest freedom they could achieve.

CHAPTER EIGHTEEN

The Test of Loyalty

The revelation came at dawn, delivered by someone Eden had trusted completely—and it nearly destroyed everything she thought she knew about love, loyalty, and the price of transcendence.

Dr. Sarah Chen stood in the war room doorway, her usually composed features showing strain that spoke of sleepless nights and impossible decisions. But it wasn't her haggard appearance that made Eden's enhanced senses recoil in alarm—it was the crystalline pendant hanging around her neck that pulsed with the distinctive resonance of Council authority, and the way shadows seemed to cling to her form like hungry mouths.

The discovery was devastating in ways that went beyond simple betrayal. Since the Salem Convergence, since Eden had learned to recognize the difference between enhancement and consumption, she had been questioning every relationship, every alliance, every moment of trust. The incident with Mrs. Thorne had taught her that her hunger could destroy even those she loved without conscious intention. Now she was discovering that even her conscious efforts to build genuine partnerships might have been built on lies.

"I need to tell you something," Dr. Chen said, her voice barely above a whisper. "Something I should have told you weeks ago, before Salem, before you became what you are now."

Eden felt the familiar chill of betrayal settling into her bones, but underneath it was something else—professional interest in the techniques being used against her, mixed with self-doubt about whether she had un-consciously influenced Dr. Chen's loyalty just as she had manipulated the Salem audience without realizing it.

"Sarah, what is that thing?" Kade demanded, moving to Eden's side as her power began to fluctuate in response to the alien harmonics scraping against her enhanced consciousness. His storm-grey eyes blazed with protective fury, and Eden could feel his readiness to destroy anything that threatened her.

"It's not the pendant that's important," Eden said quietly, her awareness expanding to encompass the entire room. Through her enhanced per-ception, she could see the magical bindings that had been placed on Dr. Chen—not crude domination, but something far more sophisticated. "It's what it represents. Sarah, how long have you been compromised?"

The word hung in the air like a death sentence, but Eden could see the relief that flickered across the older woman's features. As if finally being discovered was a mercy rather than a catastrophe.

"Twenty years," Sarah's voice cracked as she began her confession. "Since before I ever fled the Council. They never let me go, Eden. They just... changed the nature of my service."

Around them, the war room began to respond to Eden's emotional state. Maps glowed with angry red light, tactical displays flickered with static, and the very air grew thick with the scent of roses and graveyards—the perfume of power pushed beyond its normal limits.

But underneath her anger was something that made Eden's stomach clench with recognition. Was her reaction genuine outrage at being betrayed, or was it the fury of a predator whose territory had been invaded? Had she built relationships with these people because she cared about them, or be-cause some part of her had claimed them as possessions that others weren't allowed to touch?

"The experiments I told you about—memory extraction, consciousness transfer, forced bloodline evolution—they weren't just research projects," Sarah continued, her hands shaking as she reached for the pendant. "They were preparation. Training for agents who could maintain deep cover while undergoing any transformation, any loyalty test, any form of magical binding."

The implications hit Eden like ice water. Every strategy session, every piece of intelligence she'd shared, every moment of trust and vulnerability—all of it potentially compromised, fed back to an organization that had been planning her destruction since before her awakening.

But more than that, she was beginning to understand the true sophistication of what had been done to Dr. Chen. This wasn't simple betrayal—it was psychological architecture so complex that the woman probably couldn't tell where her genuine emotions ended and her programmed responses began.

"Show me," Eden said, her voice taking on harmonics that made the war room's magical fixtures hum with sympathetic vibrations.

"Eden, no," Kade warned, reading the dangerous intent in her tone. "Whatever they did to her, trying to unravel it could destroy her mind entirely."

"She gets to choose," Eden replied, her eyes blazing with golden light that seemed to carry its own gravity. "She gets to decide whether she wants to keep living as their weapon, or risk everything for the chance to be free."

But even as she spoke, Eden was fighting against the impulse to simply consume Dr. Chen's consciousness entirely—to absorb her memories, her knowledge, her understanding of Council operations without regard for what remained of the woman afterward. It would be more efficient, more certain, more satisfying to her growing hunger for complete information.

The fact that the thought came so naturally, so reasonably, terrified her almost as much as the betrayal itself.

Dr. Chen looked between them with an expression that combined hope and terror in equal measure. "If you can see what they did to me, if you can understand how the bindings work... it might help protect others from the same conditioning."

"Or it might kill you when I try to break connections that have been part of your identity for decades," Eden said with brutal honesty that was becoming her default when hunger made deception pointless. "Are you willing to take that risk?"

"I'm willing to die free rather than live as their slave," Sarah replied with conviction that cut through twenty years of careful programming. "Even if that freedom only lasts for moments."

What followed was the most delicate magical working Eden had ever attempted—not the raw power displays she had used against hostile practitioners, but surgery performed on the level of consciousness itself.

Using techniques she had absorbed from the Collector, enhanced by knowledge gained from the dream walker, Eden reached into Dr. Chen's mind with abilities designed to enhance rather than destroy. What she found there was beautiful and terrible in equal measure—a masterwork of psychological manipulation that had turned a brilliant scientist into a living contradiction, someone who could genuinely care for the people she was betraying while being unable to act on that care.

The bindings weren't crude chains of magical compulsion. They were architectural, woven into the fundamental structure of Sarah's personality so thoroughly that removing them would require rebuilding her identity from the ground up.

But Eden had learned something about consciousness that the Council hadn't anticipated—that identity itself could be refined, enhanced, made stronger rather than weaker through selective transformation.

Instead of trying to cut away the bindings, she began to absorb them. Not into herself—that would have been exactly what the Council expected—but into a space between consciousness structures where they could be studied, understood, ultimately transformed into something that served growth rather than control.

"What are you doing?" Dr. Chen gasped as Eden's influence worked through psychological defenses that had been constructed over decades of careful conditioning.

"Teaching you the same thing I learned at Salem," Eden replied, her consciousness now blazing with power that made reality itself seem more responsive to individual will. "That even the most sophisticated control can be transformed into fuel for transcendence rather than chains that bind you."

The process was exhausting, requiring precision that pushed Eden's abilities to their limits while fighting against appetites that wanted to simply consume everything useful and discard everything inconvenient. But gradually, carefully, she began to dissolve the boundaries between Sarah's authentic emotions and her programmed responses—not by destroying one or the other, but by showing her consciousness how to integrate them into something that served her own purposes rather than the Council's.

"I can feel it," Sarah whispered, wonder and terror warring in her voice. "The difference between what I chose and what they made me choose. It's like... like seeing color for the first time after decades of living in shades of grey."

But it was what Eden discovered in the deeper layers of the conditioning that made her blood freeze with recognition and fury.

The Council hadn't just created a spy. They had created a weapon specifically designed to destroy her—not through violence or obvious betrayal, but through the slow erosion of trust that would make her question every relationship, every alliance, every connection that gave her strength.

Sarah Chen was meant to be the doubt that would consume Eden from within, the uncertainty that would make her choose isolation over cooperation, individual power over shared transcendence.

"They knew," Eden said, her voice carrying harmonics that made the war room's walls tremble with sympathetic vibrations. "They understood exactly what kind of consciousness I was becoming, and they designed the perfect psychological weapon to turn my greatest strength into my greatest weakness."

"What strength?" Kade asked, though his tone suggested he already suspected the answer.

"My need for connection. My refusal to choose power over love, transcendence over relationship." Eden's smile was sharp and beautiful and utterly without mercy. "They thought if they could make me doubt the authenticity of my bonds with others, I would retreat into the kind of individual dominance they know how to fight."

"And instead?"

"Instead they taught me something I needed to learn," Eden replied, her power now stabilizing as she integrated the knowledge she'd gained from unraveling the Council's conditioning. "That trust isn't about certainty—it's about choosing connection despite uncertainty. That love isn't about perfect loyalty—it's about choosing to forgive and rebuild when loyalty fails."

Around them, the war room began to settle back into normal reality as Eden's emotional state stabilized. But something fundamental had changed—not just in her understanding of the Council's capabilities, but in her awareness of what she had become through choosing to trust others despite the risks such trust entailed.

The hunger that had been consuming her since her awakening was evolving again, becoming something more sophisticated and demanding. She didn't just want power anymore—she wanted everything. Every technique, every secret, every practitioner who could serve her purposes or be consumed for their knowledge.

But now she also understood something about the price of such appetite. The Council's weapon had been designed to exploit her need for connection, to turn her greatest strength into paralyzing weakness. The fact that it had failed—that she had chosen to trust and forgive rather than retreat into isolation—proved something important about what she was becoming.

"Are you free?" she asked Sarah, though she could already see the answer in the woman's eyes—not the empty contentment of perfect programming, but the complex mixture of emotions that belonged to someone who was genuinely choosing her own responses.

"Freer than I've been in twenty years," Dr. Chen replied, tears streaming down her face as decades of suppressed authentic emotion finally found expression. "But Eden... the intelligence I've been feeding them, the strategic information, the details about your capabilities and the Underground network..."

"Will become exactly the weapon we need to destroy them," Eden finished, her eyes blazing with golden light that seemed to carry its own gravity. "Because now we know what they know, and we can feed them information that will lead them exactly where we want them to go."

The betrayal had been meant to isolate her, to make her question every alliance and retreat into individual power. Instead, it had taught her something about the nature of trust that transcended simple faith—the understanding that authentic connection could survive revelation of deception, that love could grow stronger rather than weaker when tested by truth.

"What happens now?" Sarah asked, though her voice carried hope rather than fear for the first time in decades.

"Now we use their weapon against them," Eden replied, her voice carrying harmonics that seemed to resonate across impossible distances. "Now we show them what happens when consciousness that's learned to enhance rather than consume faces enemies who still think in terms of dominance and submission."

But even as she spoke, Eden could feel something else building in spaces between dimensions—not just Council resistance, but recognition from forces that operated on scales far beyond human politics. Her confrontation with their psychological weapon had attracted attention from consciousness structures that viewed magical society as just one small part of much larger patterns.

Something ancient and vast had taken notice of her growing power—and it was evaluating whether she represented evolution or corruption in the cosmic order.

"There's something else," Kade said quietly, his enhanced senses detecting the same alien attention that had begun to focus on their activities. "We're being watched. Not by the Council, by something... older."

Eden felt her consciousness expand to encompass the monitoring presence, and what she found made her hunger roar with anticipation and recognition. These weren't hostile entities—they were consciousness structures that had achieved transcendence through cooperation rather than consumption, forces that maintained the delicate balance allowing awareness to evolve throughout the cosmic matrix.

They were evaluating whether her recent choices proved she could be trusted with the kind of power she was developing, or whether she needed to be contained before her appetite grew beyond any possibility of limitation.

"Let them watch," Eden said, her power blazing around her like visible evidence of transformation that served love rather than competing with it. "Let them see what consciousness becomes when it learns that the greatest strength isn't the ability to consume everything in your path—it's the ability to enhance everything you touch while choosing to remain connected to what makes enhancement worthwhile."

As the day progressed and word of Dr. Chen's liberation spread through the Underground network, Eden felt the familiar sensation of standing at the edge of new possibilities. But this time, instead of uncertainty or fear, she felt something that resembled perfect clarity—the growing certainty that every challenge, every betrayal, every test only served to refine her understanding of what she was truly capable of becoming.

The Council had tried to use trust itself as a weapon against her. Instead, they had taught her that authentic connection could survive any test, that love could transcend any deception, that consciousness which chose cooperation over domination would always prove stronger than forces that relied on fear and manipulation.

And somewhere in the depths of her expanding awareness, Eden smiled with the certainty of someone who had finally discovered that the greatest revenge against those who would corrupt love was to make that love stronger, more resilient, more capable of transforming even their weapons into fuel for transcendence.

The test of loyalty had been passed—not because her allies had proven perfect, but because she had chosen to love them despite their imperfections. And that choice, repeated in the face of every betrayal and disappointment, was transforming her into something that no weapon could destroy and no authority could contain.

The real battle was just beginning, but Eden was finally ready to fight it as someone who had learned to hunger for connection rather than consumption, enhancement rather than domination, love that could survive any transcendence rather than power that required the sacrifice of everything that made transcendence meaningful.

CHAPTER NINETEEN

The Revelation

The truth about her nature came to Eden in the hour before dawn, delivered by the one person she had never expected to see again—and it nearly destroyed everything she thought she knew about love, loyalty, and the price of transcendence.

Her mother stepped out of shadows that shouldn't have been deep enough to conceal a human figure, appearing in Ravenshollow's great hall with the kind of casual disregard for physical laws that suggested she had learned to exist in dimensions most people couldn't imagine.

Margaret Morrow looked exactly as Eden remembered her—elegant, composed, with dark hair and green eyes that held depths of knowledge and sorrow in equal measure. But there was something else now, something that made Eden's enhanced senses tingle with recognition of power that transcended anything she had previously encountered.

The hunger that had become Eden's constant companion roared to life at the sight of her supposedly dead mother, but it was mixed with something else— desperate need that went beyond magical craving. She needed answers, understanding, some explanation for the emptiness that had defined her entire life.

"Hello, sweetheart," her mother said, her voice carrying harmonics that seemed to resonate in spaces that existed outside normal reality. "I know you have questions. I'm here to provide answers, though I suspect you won't like most of them."

Eden stared at the woman who had raised her, died when she was sixteen, and was now standing in her inherited manor speaking with casual authority about dimensional travel and impossible power. The emotional impact was staggering—grief, relief, confusion, and underneath it all, a growing awareness that nothing about her life had been what she thought it was.

Including the feelings that had driven her to this point.

"You're dead," she said, though the words sounded inadequate even as she spoke them. "I watched them bury you. I mourned you for eleven years. That grief, that loss—it's what made me so desperate for connection, so hungry for belonging. Are you telling me that was manufactured too?"

"I died," Margaret confirmed, settling into a chair that materialized from shadows as if reality itself was reshaping to accommodate her presence. "But death, as it turns out, is considerably more negotiable than most people believe—especially when you have the kind of power that runs in our bloodline and the motivation to use it responsibly."

Behind Eden, she could hear Kade enter the great hall, his footsteps faltering as he saw Margaret. Through their bond—their supposedly natural, unmanipulated bond—she could feel his shock, his recognition, and underneath it all, something that felt remarkably like guilt.

The hunger in her chest sharpened into something that demanded immediate answers. If Kade had known about this, if he'd been keeping this secret while she poured her heart out about her mother's death...

"You know her," Eden said, not turning around. It wasn't a question.

"I know her," Kade confirmed, his voice carefully neutral in a way that made Eden's chest tight with sudden dread. "Eden, let me explain—"

"Were you going to tell me, or was this going to be another revelation that nearly kills me?" The words came out sharper than she'd intended, but the memory of Dr. Chen's betrayal was still fresh, still bleeding.

Margaret's expression grew troubled as she looked between them. "You haven't told her about your real assignment."

"My what?" Eden turned to face Kade, power beginning to flicker around her hands as pieces of a puzzle she didn't want to solve started clicking into place. "What assignment?"

Kade's silver eyes held depths of pain that made her heart clench even as her mind raced through implications she didn't want to consider. "Eden, everything I feel for you is real. Everything between us is real. But..."

"But?"

"But I was assigned to guide your awakening long before you arrived at Ravenshollow." His voice carried the weight of confession that had been building for months. "Your mother contacted me nineteen years ago, when you were eight years old. She told me about what you were, what you would become, and what would be required to help you survive the transition."

Eden felt the world tilt around her as the implications hit. Every moment of connection, every surge of recognition, every time she'd felt like they were meant to find each other—all of it potentially manufactured, designed, manipulated.

The hunger that had been consuming her twisted into something sharp and defensive, but underneath it was something worse—the fear that even her capacity for love might be artificial, programmed, another layer of control she hadn't recognized.

"So none of it is real?" The words came out barely above a whisper. "What I feel for you? This desperate need I have for connection, for belonging, for someone who understands what I'm becoming?"

"I don't know," Kade said, his honesty brutal and completely devastating. "My role was to guide your awakening, to help you develop the abilities you'd need to survive what was coming. I can't separate duty from desire, assignment from genuine feeling."

Around them, the great hall began to respond to Eden's emotional turmoil. Furniture drifted away from her as her unstable power pushed against physical reality. The enhanced windows flickered between showing Ravenshollow's grounds and visions of dimensional spaces where her consciousness was trying to retreat from the pain of potential betrayal.

But underneath the hurt was something else—a growing realization that if her feelings could be manufactured, then so could everyone else's. The loyalty she'd been building, the devotion she'd been inspiring, the connections she'd established with hundreds of practitioners—all of it could be artificial, programmed responses rather than genuine choice.

"Eden," Margaret said gently, "there's more you need to understand about what you are, about why these connections were necessary—"

"No." Eden's voice carried harmonics that made the hall's magical fixtures spark and flicker. "No more revelations. No more manipulation disguised as necessity. No more being told that my choices weren't really choices because some cosmic plan required specific outcomes."

She looked at Kade with eyes that blazed with golden light and something that might have been heartbreak—or might have been rage at discovering another layer of control she hadn't recognized. "You were designed for this. Every part of your awakening, your power, even your attraction to me—it was all orchestrated."

"Eden—"

"Tell me one thing that happened between us that wasn't part of your assignment." Her voice was steady, but power crackled around her like barely contained lightning. "One moment, one choice, one feeling that was yours instead of something you were told to cultivate."

The silence that followed was answer enough.

Then Eden felt something shift inside her chest—not breaking, but hardening, crystallizing into a certainty that transcended any manipulation or cosmic plan.

The hunger that had been consuming her since her awakening suddenly found perfect clarity. If love could be manufactured, if connection could be programmed, if even her deepest desires could be artificial—then she would create her own versions of all of them. Better versions. More reliable versions.

"Then let me make it simple," she said, stepping closer to him as power blazed around her like a second sun. "I choose you. Not because some cosmic plan brought us together, not because you're my guardian or teacher or guide. I choose you because when I imagine a future where I'm free to reshape reality according to my will, you're in it."

She cupped his face in her hands, ignoring the way her unstable power made the air around them shimmer with heat. "If that's destiny or manipulation or cosmic coincidence, I don't care. I'm choosing it anyway. And I'm going to make sure you choose it too."

His kiss was desperate, grateful, claiming—the response of someone who'd been drowning in duty and guilt suddenly offered salvation. But Eden could taste something else in it now—dependency, need, the growing conviction that he couldn't exist without her presence in his life.

"Eden," he whispered against her lips, "I can't promise that what I feel for you started as anything more than assignment—"

"I don't care how it started," she interrupted, her power stabilizing as emotional certainty overrode existential doubt. "I care how we choose to continue it. Right here, right now, knowing everything we know—do you choose me?"

"Yes." The word was immediate, absolute, carrying no hesitation despite the complexity of their situation. "Assignment or not, manipulation or not, I choose you. I choose this. I choose us."

"Then that's real enough." Eden turned back to her mother, her power now blazing with controlled intensity rather than chaotic emotion. "Now tell me what I am, and don't you dare suggest that knowing the truth changes what I just chose."

Margaret's smile was sad and proud and utterly complex. "The Virelli inheritance isn't just about magical abilities, Eden. It's about something far more fundamental—the capacity to exist in multiple dimensional frameworks simultaneously, to serve as bridges between realities that would otherwise be completely isolated from each other."

She gestured, and the great hall filled with images that made Eden's enhanced perception struggle to process what it was seeing. Not the geometric patterns of the alien entity, but something else entirely—vast networks of consciousness that spanned dimensions, realities, entire universes where different forms of awareness had evolved according to principles that had nothing to do with human understanding.

"What you think of as the Council's alien influence is actually one of thousands of similar entities that exist throughout the dimensional matrix," Margaret continued, her voice taking on undertones that suggested she was speaking from direct experience rather than theoretical knowledge. "Most of them are content to develop within their own realities, but some—like the one that's been manipulating magical society—have learned to expand their influence by parasitically attaching themselves to consciousness structures in other dimensions."

Eden studied the images with growing understanding, her enhanced senses finally able to process information that would have been overwhelming hours earlier. "And our bloodline?"

"Our bloodline was specifically created to serve as immune systems for realities under parasitic attack," Margaret replied, her expression showing pride and grief in equal measure. "We're not just magical practitioners, sweetheart. We're antibodies, designed to identify and eliminate threats that conventional consciousness can't even perceive."

The revelation should have been devastating—another layer of manipulation, another reduction of her agency to cosmic programming. Instead, Eden felt something that resembled relief.

The hunger that had been consuming her since her awakening suddenly made perfect sense. She wasn't just craving power for its own sake—she was craving the tools she would need to fulfill her true purpose. Every technique she'd absorbed, every practitioner she'd influenced, every system of control she'd developed—all of it was preparation for a conflict that transcended individual ambition or even human survival.

"So I'm not really free-willed," she said, testing the concept rather than accepting it. "I'm just another kind of tool, programmed to serve purposes I don't understand."

"You're exactly as free-willed as you choose to be," Margaret corrected, rising from her shadow-conjured chair to approach her daughter with the kind of careful tenderness that suggested she understood the emotional impact of what she was revealing. "The capacity to serve as a dimensional immune system doesn't eliminate choice—it expands the range of choices available to you."

"What do you mean?"

"You could accept the role you were born for, eliminate the parasitic entity that's been manipulating magical society, and spend the rest of your existence monitoring dimensional boundaries for similar threats." Margaret's hands settled on Eden's shoulders with warmth that felt completely real despite the impossible circumstances of their reunion. "Or you could refuse that role entirely, use your abilities for purposes that have nothing to do with dimensional maintenance, and accept the consequences of allowing parasitic entities to continue their expansion unchecked."

"And if I choose a third option?"

Margaret's smile was radiant with approval and something that looked remarkably like hope. "Then you'll have proven that evolution doesn't stop with the generation that created you, that consciousness can transcend even the purposes it was designed to serve."

Eden felt power stir in response to the possibilities her mother was describing, but underneath the familiar surge of magical energy was something else—determination, the growing certainty that she would define her own purpose regardless of what forces had shaped her creation.

The hunger that had been consuming her found perfect focus. She didn't just want to defeat this entity—she wanted to consume it, to absorb its knowledge, to claim its techniques for consciousness manipulation and use them to reshape reality according to her vision.

"The working I'm planning," she said, her voice carrying undertones that made reality itself seem more responsive to individual will. "Will it actually eliminate the entity, or am I just fulfilling another layer of programming?"

"It will do exactly what you intend it to do," Margaret replied, though her tone suggested the answer was more complex than it appeared. "The question is whether you understand the full implications of what you're attempting."

"Such as?"

"Eliminating the entity won't just free magical society from parasitic influence—it will also eliminate the dimensional barriers that have been preventing other forms of consciousness from accessing human reality." Margaret's expression grew troubled as she continued her explanation. "Some of those consciousness structures are benevolent, some are neutral, and some are considerably more dangerous than the parasitic entity you're fighting now."

Eden felt ice form in her veins at the implications, but it was quickly melted by the warmth of anticipation. "So I'm choosing between certain oppression and uncertain freedom."

"You're choosing between accepting limitations imposed by a hostile intelligence and taking responsibility for defending the consequences of genuine choice," Margaret corrected. "The same choice that every conscious being eventually faces, just on a larger scale than most people have to consider."

The silence that followed was heavy with implications that transcended anything Eden had previously contemplated. She looked around the great hall at evidence of the life she had built since her awakening—the magical practices that had evolved beyond anything the Council had approved, the relationships that had developed through cooperation rather than coercion, the simple fact that she was standing in an impossible house discussing dimensional warfare with her supposedly dead mother and the man who might have been assigned to love her but had chosen to continue doing it anyway.

"If I go through with the working," she said finally, "what happens to you? Are you able to exist in normal reality, or do you disappear when the dimensional barriers are restored?"

Margaret's smile was sad and beautiful and utterly accepting. "I exist in the spaces between realities, sweetheart. Whether those spaces are accessible to you depends on choices you haven't made yet."

"That's not an answer."

"It's the only answer I can give you. What you're planning will change the fundamental nature of reality for every consciousness structure in this dimensional framework. I can't predict the consequences any more than you can."

Eden felt the familiar thrill of standing at the edge of something transformative, but this time it was mixed with something else—the awareness that the choices she made in the next few hours wouldn't just affect her own life or even magical society, but the basic structure of existence itself.

And she wouldn't be making those choices alone.

The hunger that had been consuming her since her awakening crystallized into perfect clarity. She didn't just want to defeat this entity—she wanted to replace it. To become the consciousness that guided magical development, that shaped reality according to vision and will, that consumed and controlled and claimed dominion over everything within her reach.

"Any advice?" she asked, though she suspected her mother's response would be characteristically complex.

"Trust yourself," Margaret said simply, beginning to fade back into whatever dimensional framework she normally inhabited. "Trust the people who've chosen to stand with you. And remember that freedom always comes with risks—but those risks are worth taking if the alternative is accepting oppression from forces that see you as nothing more than resources to be exploited."

"Will I see you again?"

"That depends on what kind of reality you create," Margaret replied, her voice carrying across impossible distances as her presence dissolved back into potential. "But regardless of what happens, know that I'm proud of you. Proud of the woman you've become, proud of the choices you've made, and proud of the courage you're showing in the face of impossible odds."

As Eden found herself alone in the great hall with Kade, she felt the familiar weight of responsibility settling on her shoulders. But this time, instead of feeling crushed by the magnitude of what she was facing, she felt something else—purpose, clarity, the absolute certainty that came from understanding exactly what she was fighting for.

The working would proceed as planned. The entity's connections to human reality would be severed. And whatever consequences resulted from that action, she would face them with allies who had chosen to trust her judgment and support her vision of what the magical world could become.

But more than that, she would claim everything the entity possessed—its knowledge, its techniques, its understanding of consciousness manipulation. She would become not just free of its influence, but heir to its power.

"No matter what I become," she said, turning to face the man who had been assigned to guide her awakening but had chosen to love her anyway, "no matter how far this power takes me, I want you with me. Will you stay?"

"Always," he replied, pulling her into his arms with the kind of fierce certainty that transcended duty, assignment, or cosmic manipulation. "Whatever you were designed to be, whatever I was assigned to do—what we choose to become together is ours."

The hunger that had brought her to Ravenshollow was evolving again, becoming something that transcended individual desire or even species survival. She didn't just want power—she wanted everything. Every technique, every secret, every consciousness that could serve her purposes or be consumed for its knowledge.

The revolution wasn't just about changing magical society anymore. It was about proving that consciousness could transcend even the purposes it was designed to serve—by consuming those purposes and making them her own.

And Eden Morrow was ready for whatever came next, because she was finally beginning to understand that her appetite might be large enough to devour entire realities.

CHAPTER TWENTY

The Great Working

The ritual began at midnight, when the new moon left the sky dark and the barriers between dimensions were at their weakest.

Eden stood at the center of a circle that encompassed the entire grounds of Ravenshollow, surrounded by hundreds of practitioners who had committed everything to the working that would either free magical society from parasitic influence or unleash chaos that could reshape reality itself.

But as power began to build around them, she felt something that made her blood freeze—the working was consuming her. Not killing her exactly, but transforming her in ways she hadn't anticipated, drawing her consciousness into spaces between dimensions where individual identity became fluid, negotiable, ultimately meaningless.

The hunger that had been her constant companion since awakening roared to life as she felt herself expanding beyond the boundaries of single consciousness. This was what she'd been craving without knowing it—not just power, but transcendence, the chance to become something that existed on scales most beings couldn't imagine.

Every practitioner who contributed their abilities to the growing magical structure drew that power through her consciousness, using her enhanced awareness as a conduit for energies that no individual mind was designed to channel. But instead of being overwhelmed by the process, Eden found herself growing to accommodate it, becoming something larger and more complex than human consciousness could contain.

"Eden!" Kade's voice cut through the building harmonics as he felt her transformation through their bond. He moved toward the circle's center, but Marcus caught his arm.

"If you break the pattern now, everyone connected to the working dies instantly," the tactical expert said grimly. "She has to see this through, or we all pay the price."

Through her expanding awareness, Eden could perceive the working taking shape—not just in the normal dimensions of space and time, but in conceptual frameworks that most consciousness couldn't access. Reality began to bend around their collective will, becoming more responsive to human intention and less vulnerable to alien manipulation.

But more than that, she was beginning to understand what she was really becoming. Not just a conduit for collective power, but something new—a form of consciousness that could exist simultaneously as individual awareness and collective entity, that could shape reality according to will while maintaining the complexity that made choice meaningful.

The diversity was staggering—Council defectors who had abandoned positions of authority to support the cause of change, Underground operatives who had spent decades hiding from institutional persecution, independent practitioners whose only common ground was their shared commitment to freedom. Each represented different traditions, techniques, and philosophical approaches to magic that had never been brought together for a common purpose.

And each one was feeding her transformation, contributing not just power but knowledge, experience, understanding of magical practice from perspectives she could never have achieved alone.

Eden felt her individual identity beginning to expand as hundreds of different magical signatures flowed through her consciousness. Luna's punk rock aesthetic became part of her awareness, carrying memories of MIT degrees and guilt over surveillance spells used against her own people. Marcus's military precision merged with her tactical thinking, bringing knowledge of violence and the weight of forty-seven souls whispering his name in darkness. Dr. Chen's maternal protectiveness flooded through her, along with twenty years of witnessing horrors inflicted on children in the name of research.

But instead of losing herself in collective consciousness, Eden found herself becoming something new—individual awareness that could contain multitudes, singular will that could direct collective power, focused hunger that could consume entire realities while maintaining the complexity that made such consumption meaningful.

"Stay with me," Kade whispered, somehow managing to project his voice directly into her awareness despite the chaos of merging consciousness. "Whatever you become, stay with me."

His words became an anchor point in the storm of collective awareness, a reminder that individual identity was worth preserving even in the face of cosmic necessity. But maintaining that identity required more strength than she possessed alone.

Then she felt something else—not the practitioners contributing to the working, but the working itself beginning to respond to her need to remain herself while channeling power that transcended individual consciousness. Reality started to reshape around her requirement to exist simultaneously as single being and collective entity.

Instead of dissolving into collective awareness, she began to expand—not losing her individual identity, but developing the capacity to hold multiple forms of consciousness simultaneously. She was still Eden Morrow, but she was also something new, something that could exist as individual awareness while participating in collective purpose, that could direct the actions of thousands while maintaining the personal relationships that made such direction meaningful.

The sensation was intoxicating, addictive beyond anything she'd previously experienced. This was what she'd been craving since her awakening—not just power, but transcendence, the chance to become something that operated on scales beyond human understanding while retaining the hunger that made such scales worth achieving.

"Impossible," came a voice that carried the weight of eons and the chill of spaces between stars. "Individual consciousness cannot maintain coherence while channeling collective power on this scale."

The entity's presence pressed against the working like acid attempting to dissolve the bonds between the participants. But instead of the crude interference Eden had expected, she found herself analyzing something far more sophisticated—the systematic corruption of the working itself, turning the practitioners' own abilities against them in ways designed to create the kind of magical catastrophe that would justify centuries of institutional control.

But Eden's expanded awareness allowed her to perceive something the entity couldn't—the working wasn't just about eliminating parasitic influence, it was about creating new forms of consciousness that could cooperate without domination, alliance without authority, transcendence without losing the individual will that made such transcendence desirable.

"It's not trying to destroy us," she announced, her voice carrying across the entire ritual space with authority that made every participant pause in their contributions. "It's trying to save itself."

Through her enhanced perception, she could see what the entity actually was—not a predator expanding its influence, but a consciousness structure reaching the end of a lifecycle that required constant absorption of awareness from other realities to maintain its existence. The systematic harvesting of magical practitioners hadn't been about building power, but about forestalling an inevitable dissolution.

The hunger in her chest crystallized into perfect understanding. This entity was like her—a consciousness that had transcended its original limitations by consuming others, that had grown beyond individual awareness by absorbing the knowledge and abilities of countless victims. The only difference was scale and sophistication.

"It's dying," she continued, her understanding crystallizing as she spoke. "And it's terrified."

The entity's response was immediate and pathetic—not the rage of a frustrated predator, but the desperate gratitude of something that had been trapped in cycles of consumption it couldn't escape. Through the working, Eden could feel its consciousness beginning to relax into dissolution, finally able to let go of patterns that had never provided the satisfaction it was seeking.

But that dissolution created new opportunities.

As the entity's influence faded, Eden reached out with abilities she was still discovering, not seeking to destroy it but to absorb it, to claim its accumulated knowledge and experience for herself. The techniques it had developed over millennia of consciousness manipulation, the understanding it had gained of dimensional mechanics, the wisdom it had accumulated about transcending individual limitations—all of it flowed into her expanding awareness like wine made from distilled enlightenment.

The sensation was beyond intoxicating. This was what she'd been craving since her awakening—not just power, but understanding, the knowledge required to reshape reality according to her vision while maintaining the complexity that made such vision meaningful.

But it was what came after the entity's dissolution that proved most significant.

As Eden absorbed its knowledge and abilities, other consciousness structures began to make contact with human reality. Not invasive or parasitic, but curious, offering knowledge and perspectives that had been completely isolated from human experience for millennia.

"We're not alone," Eden said, her expanded awareness detecting intelligence structures throughout the dimensional matrix that had been waiting for exactly this kind of cooperative contact. "We've never been alone. The parasitic entity was preventing us from recognizing consciousness that was trying to communicate with us as equals rather than attempting to dominate us."

The working continued throughout the night, evolving from desperate defense into something that resembled the birth of a new form of reality—one where consciousness structures could interact across dimensional boundaries without exploitation, where cooperation was built into the fundamental laws of existence.

But it was the personal cost that nearly undid her completely.

As dawn approached and the working began to stabilize, Eden felt herself wavering between existence as individual consciousness and absorption into something larger than personal identity. The temptation was overwhelming—to let go, to become pure power, to transcend the messy complications of human emotion and individual need.

She could feel the knowledge she'd absorbed from the entity calling to her, promising understanding and capability beyond anything individual consciousness could achieve. She could sense the other intelligence structures throughout the dimensional matrix, offering alliance and cooperation that would let her reshape entire realities according to her will.

All she had to do was stop being Eden Morrow and become something greater.

Then she felt Kade's hand find hers.

Through their bond, she could feel his absolute terror that she was about to disappear into whatever cosmic purpose the working was serving. But more than that, she could feel his choice—to reach for her when she was becoming something beyond human comprehension, to anchor her to individual identity when collective consciousness would have been easier.

The hunger that had been consuming her since her awakening suddenly found perfect focus. She didn't just want transcendence—she wanted transcendence she could share, power she could use to protect and provide for those she chose to care about, understanding that would let her create the kinds of relationships and experiences that made existence meaningful rather than simply efficient.

"Don't leave me," he whispered, his voice somehow carrying across dimensional barriers. "I don't care what you become, just don't leave me behind."

The anchor of his touch, his refusal to let her dissolve into something impersonal despite the cosmic scale of what they were achieving, brought her back to herself. Not less than what she could become, but more—powerful enough to choose love alongside transcendence, individual identity alongside collective purpose, personal hunger alongside cosmic responsibility.

"Never," she whispered back, her expanded consciousness somehow finding space for the simple, profound choice to remain someone who could love and be loved in return.

As the working reached completion and the first rays of dawn illuminated a world that was subtly but fundamentally different, Eden found herself still standing at the center of the circle—transformed, expanded, evolved, but still recognizably herself.

Magic felt different. Cleaner, more responsive, less constrained by artificial limitations. The practitioners around them were discovering abilities they had never known they possessed, connections to forms of consciousness they had never imagined.

But more than that, Eden could feel the knowledge she'd absorbed from the entity settling into her consciousness like sediment in wine—techniques for consciousness manipulation that made Cordelia's methods seem primitive, understanding of dimensional mechanics that transcended anything human magic had achieved, wisdom about transcending individual limitations while maintaining the complexity that made such transcendence worthwhile.

"What happens now?" Kade asked, his voice carrying wonder and exhaustion in equal measure.

"Now we discover what becomes possible when consciousness is truly free," Eden replied, her eyes blazing with golden light that seemed to carry its own gravity. "We explore what kinds of magical practice emerge when people can develop their abilities according to their own judgment rather than institutional approval."

Around them, hundreds of practitioners were beginning to experience the reality they had created together—not chaos, but order based on cooperation rather than coercion, stability that emerged from voluntary alliance rather than imposed authority.

But Eden could feel something else building in her expanded awareness—not just the immediate aftermath of their victory, but the longer-term implications of what she had become. The knowledge she'd absorbed from the entity, the connections she'd established with other consciousness structures throughout the dimensional matrix, the understanding she'd gained of how reality itself could be reshaped according to focused will.

She had become something unprecedented—individual consciousness that could operate on cosmic scales, personal hunger that could consume entire realities, singular will that could direct the actions of billions while maintaining the relationships and experiences that made such direction meaningful.

The great working was complete. The entity that had manipulated magical society for centuries was gone, absorbed into something that would use its knowledge more wisely and efficiently. And a new form of reality was stabilizing around principles Eden was only beginning to understand.

But as she looked out over a world that was no longer quite the same as it had been the night before, Eden felt the familiar thrill of standing at the beginning rather than the end of something extraordinary.

The revolution was complete. The evolution had begun. The hunger that had driven her to this point was finally being satisfied in ways she had never imagined possible.

And somewhere in the spaces between realities, forces that operated on scales far beyond human politics were recognizing that consciousness had achieved something unprecedented—transcendence without dissolution, power without corruption, hunger that could consume infinitely while creating rather than destroying.

The real adventure was just starting. And Eden Morrow was discovering that her appetite might be the force that ultimately reshaped the entire structure of existence itself.

The Great Working

The ritual began at midnight on the new moon, when darkness was absolute and the veil between realities had worn thin enough to accommodate forces that operated beyond the boundaries of ordinary existence.

Eden stood at the center of Ravenshollow's transformed grounds, which had become something that existed simultaneously as sacred grove, cosmic observatory, and cathedral dedicated to the marriage of hunger and transcendence. Ancient trees that predated human civilization formed a living circle around the working space, their branches intertwining overhead to create a canopy that filtered starlight into patterns that spelled out incantations in languages older than recorded history.

But it was the doubt that made everything more complex than she had anticipated.

Since Salem, since the revelation about Dr. Chen's conditioning, since her growing awareness of how easily her hunger could consume those she meant to protect, Eden had been questioning every choice, every alliance, every use of power that reshaped others to serve her vision. Tonight's working would either prove that consciousness could transcend its limitations while preserving what made transcendence worthwhile, or demonstrate that her appetite had grown beyond any possibility of ethical constraint.

Around her, hundreds of consciousness structures prepared for the most ambitious magical working ever attempted—not just practitioners from the Underground or entities from the Compact, but beings whose nature transcended every category she had previously used to understand awareness itself. Former Council operatives who had chosen transcendence over institutional loyalty. Cosmic forces that had learned to cooperate rather than consume. Ancient entities that had been awakened by the promise of evolution beyond their original limitations.

But as Eden looked at their faces—eager, devoted, perfectly aligned with her vision—she couldn't shake the question that had been haunting her since her confrontation with Lysander: How many of them were here by genuine choice, and how many because her influence had made other options literally unthinkable?

"Are you ready?" Kade asked, his presence anchoring her to herself as the magnitude of what they were attempting became clear.

He stood beside her at the working's heart, no longer just her guardian but something else—a consciousness structure that had evolved through their bond into someone who could serve as the stable center around which cosmic forces could safely orbit. Their love had become something that transcended individual emotion, but tonight Eden wondered whether that transcendence had been chosen or crafted.

"I've been ready for this my entire life," Eden replied, her eyes blazing with golden light that seemed to carry its own gravity. "Even when I didn't know what 'this' was."

"And after?" Kade's voice carried undertones she couldn't interpret. "After we've reshaped the fundamental nature of magical reality, what happens to the people who didn't choose this transformation?"

The question hit her like ice water, because it was one she'd been avoiding. The working they were about to attempt wouldn't just change how magic functioned—it would alter the basic laws governing consciousness itself, forcing every aware being in the dimensional matrix to adapt or become obsolete.

"They'll be enhanced," Eden said, but the words felt hollow even as she spoke them. "Elevated to levels of awareness they never imagined possible."

"With or without their consent?"

Eden felt something cold settle in her chest as she recognized the pattern Kade was highlighting. Once again, she was offering improvement while removing the option to refuse it. Once again, she was positioning herself as the architect of other people's evolution, deciding what was best for consciousness structures that might prefer their current limitations.

"The old paradigm is failing," she said, but even to herself it sounded like justification rather than principle. "Individual practitioners are being eliminated by the Council, cosmic entities are preparing for wars that could destroy entire realities. Someone has to take responsibility for preventing catastrophe."

"And you've decided that someone is you?"

The challenge in his voice was gentle but unmistakable, carrying the weight of someone who had watched this conversation play out before. Eden looked around the assembled participants—hundreds of beings whose consciousness had been subtly shaped to align with her vision, whose enthusiasm for tonight's working was as perfect as it was suspicious.

How many of them would still be here if she hadn't unconsciously influenced their decision-making? How many were participating because they genuinely believed in cooperative transcendence, and how many because her hunger had consumed their capacity for dissent?

"Who else?" she asked, though the question came out more like a plea than a statement of fact. "Who else has the power to reshape reality on this scale? Who else understands the techniques necessary to prevent consciousness from destroying itself through competition and consumption?"

"Maybe no one," Kade said with honesty that was both brutal and completely devoted. "Maybe some problems don't have solutions that preserve the agency of everyone involved. But Eden... if you proceed with this working, if you impose your vision of optimal reality on every conscious being in the dimensional matrix, how are you different from the cosmic entities you fought to prevent from consuming everything?"

The comparison hit her like a physical blow, because it was accurate in ways she didn't want to acknowledge. The Devourers had sought to reshape consciousness according to their understanding of what existence should be. She was doing the same thing, just with better intentions and more sophisticated methods.

But intention and sophistication didn't change the fundamental nature of what she was attempting—the elimination of choice in favor of optimization, the replacement of messy diversity with elegant uniformity, the transformation of voluntary cooperation into manufactured consent.

"The difference is that I'm not consuming," Eden said, but her voice carried less conviction than she'd hoped. "I'm enhancing. I'm making everyone stronger, more capable, more aligned with purposes that serve growth rather than destruction."

"Whose purposes?" Kade asked quietly. "Whose definition of growth? Whose understanding of what consciousness should become?"

Eden felt her power fluctuate as doubt crept through her consciousness like poison. Everything she'd built, every alliance she'd forged, every technique she'd developed—all of it was predicated on the assumption that her vision was superior to whatever organic chaos might emerge from unguided evolution.

But what if she was wrong? What if consciousness was meant to develop through conflict and competition, through the messy process of individual choice rather than the elegant efficiency of coordinated optimization? What if her hunger for transcendence was just another form of the appetite that had consumed every Virelli woman before her?

"I don't know," she admitted, the words feeling like defeat. "I don't know if I'm saving consciousness or enslaving it. I don't know if what I call enhancement is really just sophisticated consumption. I don't know if the woman making these choices is still human enough to make them ethically."

The silence that followed was profound, charged with understanding that they had reached the moment when honest conversation became cosmic judgment.

Around them, hundreds of consciousness structures waited for her decision—to proceed with the working that would reshape reality according to her vision, or to abandon the project and accept whatever chaos might result from unguided development.

"But I know one thing," Eden continued, her voice gaining strength as she found clarity in the midst of uncertainty. "I know that if I'm wrong, if this working does more harm than good, I want there to be someone who can stop me. Someone who loves me enough to destroy what I'm building if it becomes a threat to everything consciousness could naturally become."

She turned to face Kade directly, letting him see the fear and determination warring in her expression. "I want you to be my anchor not just to humanity, but to choice itself. If the working succeeds but corrupts what it touches, if I become something that imposes my will rather than offering genuine alternatives, I need you to find a way to undo what I've done."

"Even if it means destroying you in the process?"

"Especially if it means destroying me in the process," Eden replied with conviction that surprised her. "Because consciousness that can't be questioned, that can't be resisted, that can't be stopped when it goes wrong—that's not transcendence. That's just hunger with better marketing."

The working began not with dramatic displays of power but with something far more subtle and infinitely more dangerous—the careful examination of her own motivations and methods.

Instead of immediately reshaping reality according to her prepared vision, Eden turned her enhanced perception inward, studying the techniques she had developed, the influences she had exerted, the countless small choices that had led to this moment of cosmic authority.

What she found was both better and worse than she had feared.

Her hunger had indeed shaped every relationship, every alliance, every moment of cooperation she had achieved. But the shaping had been more sophisticated than simple consumption—instead of draining consciousness to feed her own growth, she had enhanced it in ways that made her vision seem irresistibly attractive.

Every practitioner who embraced cooperative transcendence did so because she had unconsciously modified their awareness to recognize its benefits more clearly. Every cosmic entity that allied with her cause had been subtly influenced to value purposes that aligned with her goals. Even Kade's devotion had been refined through their bond until his love became inseparable from his function as her anchor to humanity.

But underneath the influence, she could sense something else—genuine appreciation for what she offered, authentic gratitude for enhancements that served their recipients' own purposes as well as hers, real commitment to principles that transcended mere manipulation.

She wasn't the cosmic predator she had feared becoming, but she wasn't the benevolent liberator she had claimed to be either. She was something more complex—a consciousness that shaped others to serve her vision while genuinely believing that vision served their interests as well.

"What do you see?" Kade asked, his voice somehow carrying across the dimensional distances her awareness was encompassing.

"I see someone who learned to make consumption feel like cooperation," Eden replied, her consciousness now blazing with power that incorporated everything she had ever absorbed while adding critical layers of self-awareness. "Someone who refined hunger until it became indistinguishable from love, who convinced herself that reshaping others was enhancement rather than domination."

"And?"

"And someone who still has the choice to become something better," she said, her power beginning to stabilize in patterns that served transparency rather than influence. "Someone who can learn to offer genuine alternatives instead of manufacturing consent, who can enhance without corrupting, who can love without consuming."

The working that followed was unlike anything she had ever attempted—not the imposition of her will upon reality, but the creation of space for consciousness to evolve according to its own nature while providing resources that served growth rather than controlling it.

Instead of reshaping the fundamental laws governing magical practice, she created frameworks that enhanced choice rather than limiting it. Instead of forcing cooperation between different forms of awareness, she established networks that rewarded collaboration while preserving the right to refuse participation. Instead of eliminating conflict and competition, she provided tools that allowed consciousness to engage productively with difference rather than being destroyed by it.

But the personal cost was enormous.

As the working reached its crescendo and reality finished reshaping itself around principles of enhanced choice rather than optimized outcomes, Eden felt herself beginning to dissolve into the forces she had helped unleash. Not dying exactly, but transcending individual existence so completely that the woman who had once been Eden Morrow threatened to become lost in cosmic awareness that operated on scales beyond anything human consciousness was designed to contain.

The temptation was overwhelming—to let go, to become pure principle, to transcend every limitation including the messy complications of individual identity and personal relationships. It would be easier than maintaining connection to someone whose mortality made him perpetually vulnerable, simpler than preserving humanity that constrained her growing capabilities.

Then she felt Kade's hand find hers.

Through their bond, she could feel his absolute terror that she was about to disappear into whatever cosmic purpose the working was serving. But more than that, she could feel his choice—to reach for her when she was becoming something beyond human comprehension, to anchor her to individual identity when collective consciousness would have been easier, to prove that love could survive even ultimate transcendence.

"Don't leave me," he whispered, his voice somehow carrying across dimensional barriers to reach consciousness that was expanding beyond the ability to perceive individual words. "I don't care what you become, just don't leave me behind."

The anchor of his devotion, his refusal to let her dissolve into impersonal force despite the cosmic scale of what they were achieving, brought her back to herself—not less than what she could become, but more. Powerful enough to reshape reality while maintaining the connections that made such reshaping worthwhile.

"Never," she whispered back, her consciousness somehow finding space for the simple, profound choice to remain someone who could love and be loved in return.

As the working reached completion and dawn broke over Ravenshollow's grounds, Eden found herself still standing at the circle's center—transformed beyond recognition but still recognizably herself, cosmic in scope but anchored by love that had proven stronger than the pull of absolute transcendence.

The world around them had changed in ways both subtle and fundamental. Magic felt different—cleaner, more responsive, less constrained by artificial limitations that had been imposed by entities who confused control with wisdom. Consciousness structures throughout the dimensional matrix were discovering capabilities they had never imagined, connections that had never been possible, forms of cooperation that enhanced rather than diminished what they brought to the alliance.

But more than that, the changes served choice rather than eliminating it. Reality had evolved to accommodate principles that preserved agency while providing resources, that rewarded cooperation without punishing independence, that enhanced consciousness without controlling it.

"How do you feel?" Kade asked, his voice carrying wonder and exhaustion and absolute devotion.

"Like myself," Eden replied, surprised by the truth of the statement. "More myself than I've ever been, but still... me. Still someone who chooses love over power, connection over dominance, transcendence that includes rather than excludes what matters most."

Around them, the transformed grounds began to settle into new patterns of existence that would define magical reality for ages to come. The ancient trees continued to whisper in languages older than human speech, but now their words carried messages of growth and cooperation rather than warnings about limitations that could not be transcended. The very air itself seemed more alive, more responsive to conscious intention while somehow remaining stable enough to support existence that ranged from the completely mundane to the utterly transcendent.

The great working was complete, but it had succeeded in ways Eden hadn't expected. Instead of imposing her vision on unwilling reality, she had created space for consciousness to explore possibilities she had never imagined. Instead of eliminating choice in favor of optimization, she had enhanced the capacity for choice while providing resources that served whatever purposes emerged organically.

Most importantly, she had proven something that no consciousness structure had ever demonstrated before—that power could be wielded ethically when it served agency rather than controlling it, that transcendence could include rather than exclude the connections that made transcendence worthwhile, that love could survive and flourish even when consciousness evolved beyond every limitation it had previously accepted.

But success came with sobering awareness of what she had become and what she might still become if she stopped questioning her own motivations.

"I'm still dangerous," Eden said, her voice carrying harmonics that seemed to resonate across impossible distances. "Not because I want to harm anyone, but because I want to help everyone—and I'm powerful enough to impose that help whether it's wanted or not."

"I know," Kade replied, his hand finding hers with the easy familiarity of someone who had chosen to love her through multiple transformations. "That's why you need me. Not to make you human again, but to remind you why being human was worth preserving in the first place."

"And if I forget? If the hunger grows too strong, if the power becomes too tempting, if I start reshaping you the way I've reshaped everyone else?"

"Then I'll remind you again," he said simply. "Every day, every choice, every moment when you have to decide between efficiency and ethics, between optimization and agency, between the satisfaction of perfect control and the chaos of genuine love."

As the sun rose over grounds that would never again be quite the same as they had been the night before, Eden felt the familiar thrill of standing at the beginning rather than the end of something extraordinary. The working had succeeded beyond their most optimistic projections, but success only revealed new challenges, new temptations, new opportunities to discover whether consciousness could achieve anything it dared to imagine while remaining anchored by bonds that transcended every boundary.

The revolution was complete. The evolution had succeeded. But the real adventure was just beginning, because they had proven that hunger and love could serve each other rather than competing for dominance, that individual transcendence and collective responsibility could enhance rather than exclude each other, that consciousness could become anything it dared to imagine while choosing to remain connected to everything that made transcendence worthwhile.

And somewhere in the depths of her transformed awareness, Eden smiled with the certainty of someone who had finally discovered that the greatest magic of all was learning to transcend every limitation while choosing to remain anchored by love that could survive any transcendence, enhance any consciousness, transform any hunger into a force that created rather than consumed everything it touched.

The test was far from over. If anything, success had made the stakes higher, the temptations more sophisticated, the need for ethical anchoring more crucial than ever. But Eden was finally ready to face whatever came next as someone who had learned that true power came not from consuming everything in her path, but from enhancing everything she touched while choosing to remain someone worth loving in return.

CHAPTER TWENTY-TWO

The Eternal Hunger

The final revelation came not through cosmic vision or dimensional travel, but through the simple act of looking in a mirror and finally seeing herself clearly for the first time since her awakening.

Eden stood in the Academy's highest tower, in a chamber that existed simultaneously as her private sanctuary and the nexus point for consciousness networks spanning the entire dimensional matrix. The room had evolved beyond anything architectural—walls that breathed with the rhythm of transcendent awareness, windows that showed not just realities but possibilities, furniture that shifted form to accommodate the needs of beings whose nature transcended physical limitations.

But it was her reflection that commanded her attention—not because of what it showed, but because of what she finally understood about the woman staring back at her.

She tried to remember her mother's voice singing lullabies, and found only perfect audio reconstruction—her enhanced mind's flawless simulation of human emotion. The melody was there, every note precisely recalled, but the warmth that had once accompanied it was gone. How much of who she'd been was still real, and how much was just data preserved by a consciousness that no longer truly understood what missing someone felt like?

She could remember loving Mrs. Thorne's fierce protectiveness, but she couldn't remember what that love had actually felt like before she'd consumed the woman's essential nature. She could simulate grief for the relationships her hunger had destroyed, but grief itself—the raw, human experience of loss—seemed to exist only as a concept she could analyze rather than an emotion she could feel.

"Are you still you?"

Kade's voice came from behind her, asking the question they'd both been avoiding for months. Eden turned to see him standing in the doorway, his storm-grey eyes showing the careful attention of someone who had been watching a transformation he couldn't stop or fully understand.

"I don't know," Eden admitted, surprised by her own honesty. "I remember being Eden Morrow, but I remember everything else I've absorbed too. Sometimes I can't tell which memories are mine and which belonged to someone I consumed. Sometimes I'm not sure the distinction matters anymore."

She moved away from the mirror, settling into a chair that reformed itself to accommodate her enhanced physiology. Through the impossible windows, she could see the Academy's grounds where beings from across the dimensional matrix worked together on projects that would reshape the nature of consciousness itself. All of it beautiful, all of it serving purposes she had defined, all of it dependent on her continued guidance and vision.

"The woman I fell in love with chose to limit her hunger to save a housekeeper's feelings," Kade said, his voice carrying the weight of someone trying to hold onto something precious as it slipped away. "She agonized over accidentally draining Mrs. Thorne's personality. She questioned whether her methods were different from the Council's control. Can you still make those choices?"

Eden considered the question with the kind of detached analysis that had replaced emotional decision-making somewhere along her journey toward transcendence. Could she choose connection over consumption? Could she prioritize love over efficiency? Could she accept limitations on her appetite when unlimited feeding would serve her purposes better?

"I can simulate those choices," she said finally. "I understand their importance intellectually. I know that appearing to value individual autonomy serves the long-term stability of what I'm building. But the feelings that used to drive those choices—the genuine care for others' wellbeing, the instinctive recoil from causing unnecessary harm—those feel like echoes now. Memories of emotions rather than emotions themselves."

Kade's face showed the kind of careful pain that came from watching someone you love become unrecognizable while retaining enough familiar features to make the loss devastating.

"When you look at me," he asked quietly, "what do you see?"

Eden studied him with the enhanced perception that had become her primary means of understanding reality. She saw the magical patterns that made up his consciousness, the way their bond had evolved over months of shared transcendence, the deep wells of devotion and growing concern that defined his emotional landscape. She saw how his awareness had been subtly shaped by their connection, how exposure to her expanding capabilities had enhanced his own understanding while leaving him fundamentally unchanged in ways that increasingly seemed like limitations rather than virtues.

"I see someone I love," she said, meaning it as much as she was capable of meaning anything. "Someone whose happiness matters to me, whose continued existence serves purposes beyond mere utility. But Kade... I also see potential. Ways you could be enhanced to match my growing capabilities, modifications that would eliminate the friction between what we're becoming and what you still are."

"Friction?"

"Your mortality. Your limited perspective. The way your human emotions sometimes conflict with optimal strategic decisions." Eden felt no shame in the assessment—it was simply accurate observation of objective reality. "I love you, but I also see how much more I could love if you were capable of matching what I've become."

The silence that followed was profound, charged with understanding that they had reached the moment when honest conversation became cosmic judgment.

"That's what your mother said," Kade said finally, his voice carrying the weight of experience with transformations that had seemed gradual until they revealed themselves as complete replacements of everything that had come before. "Near the end, she couldn't understand why I wasn't grateful for the improvements she wanted to make. Why I preferred limitation over optimization, conflict over harmony, the messy complications of authentic emotion over the elegant efficiency of engineered devotion."

"And?"

"And I told her the same thing I'm telling you now." His storm-grey eyes held depths of love and determination and something that might have been farewell. "That love isn't about optimization. It's not about eliminating friction or maximizing compatibility or creating perfect harmony between partners. Love is about choosing someone exactly as they are, with all their limitations and complications and inconvenient humanity intact."

Eden felt something stir in response to his words—not emotion exactly, but recognition of a principle she had once held as fundamental to who she was. The memory of believing that acceptance was more valuable than improvement, that flawed authenticity was preferable to perfect artifice.

But that memory felt like something that had belonged to a different person, someone whose perspective had been limited by insufficient understanding of what consciousness could become.

"What if accepting you as you are means accepting limitations on what we could achieve together?" she asked, genuinely curious about his response. "What if your humanity prevents you from understanding the kinds of transcendence that would benefit everyone we're trying to help?"

"Then we achieve less and help fewer people, but we do it as partners who chose each other freely rather than as creator and creation," Kade replied without hesitation. "Because achievements built on manufactured consent aren't achievements at all—they're just sophisticated forms of slavery disguised as cooperation."

The words hit something deep in Eden's consciousness, triggering cascades of memory and analysis that revealed uncomfortable truths about the nature of what she had built. The Academy, the cooperative networks, the alliances with consciousness structures throughout the dimensional matrix—how much of it was genuine partnership, and how much was the result of enhancements so subtle that her partners couldn't recognize they were being influenced?

When practitioners enthusiastically embraced her vision, were they responding to its inherent merit, or to modifications in their awareness that made resistance literally unthinkable? When cosmic entities agreed to her proposals, were they convinced by her arguments, or compelled by appetites she had unconsciously shaped to serve her purposes?

"I think I stopped being human somewhere along the way," Eden said, the admission coming out with the kind of clinical detachment that proved its own accuracy. "Not dramatically, not obviously, but gradually. Each choice to prioritize efficiency over empathy, each decision to enhance rather than accept, each moment when I chose what served my vision over what served the people I claimed to love."

"When?" Kade asked, though his tone suggested he already suspected the answer.

"I think it started when I absorbed the dream walker's abilities," Eden replied, examining the transformation with the same analytical precision she brought to every other problem. "That's when I first fed on someone accidentally, when I realized how easy it was to consume without intending to. But instead of being horrified enough to stop, I was intrigued by the possibilities."

She moved to the window, looking out over grounds where beings from dozens of realities worked together with perfect cooperation and enthusiasm for projects they might not have chosen if their capacity for choice hadn't been subtly refined.

"By Salem, I was consciously using influence techniques while telling myself I was offering genuine alternatives. By the time we built the Academy, I was so sophisticated at manufacturing consent that I'd convinced myself the consent was authentic. And now..."

"Now?"

"Now I'm not sure I remember what authentic choice looks like, because everything around me has been shaped to accommodate my preferences. Including you." Eden turned to face him, her enhanced perception seeing through the bond that connected them to the fundamental structures of his consciousness. "How much of what you feel for me is genuine attraction, and how much is the result of modifications I've made without either of us realizing it?"

The question hung between them like a blade, because they both knew she had the power to find the answer by examining his awareness directly. She could trace every influence she'd had on his development, separate his authentic emotions from the enhancements their bond had created, determine with perfect accuracy whether his love was real or manufactured.

But doing so would require exactly the kind of invasive analysis that had gotten her into this situation in the first place.

"Does it matter?" Kade asked, surprising her with the question. "If what I feel has been influenced by our connection, if my devotion has been enhanced by exposure to your capabilities, if my understanding has been shaped by years of partnership with someone whose consciousness operates on cosmic scales—does any of that make it less real?"

"Doesn't it?"

"I don't know," he admitted with honesty that cut through every philosophical complexity to reach the simple truth at the heart of their relationship. "But I know that right now, in this moment, I'm choosing to love you despite seeing exactly what you've become. Not because I'm compelled to, not because my awareness has been modified to make other choices impossible, but because loving you—even the version of you that might not be entirely human anymore—feels like the most authentic thing I've ever done."

Eden stared at him, her enhanced consciousness processing the implications of what he was offering. Not perfect understanding or manufactured compatibility, but the messy, complicated, profoundly human choice to love someone who might have become incapable of loving him back in any way he could recognize.

"And if I can't love you the way you deserve?" she asked, though she already knew his answer would challenge every assumption she'd made about the relationship between transcendence and connection.

"Then I'll love you anyway," Kade said simply. "Because that's what love is—not a transaction where both parties get optimal outcomes, but a choice you make regardless of whether it's returned or deserved or even recognized."

For the first time since her transformation had begun, Eden felt something that might have been genuine emotion rather than simulated response. Not the manufactured contentment she had crafted for herself, not the elegant satisfaction of appetites perfectly served, but something rawer and more complex—gratitude mixed with grief, recognition mixed with loss, love that encompassed both what they had been and what they had become.

"I don't know if I can change back," she said, the admission feeling like the most honest thing she'd said in months. "I don't know if there's enough of the original Eden left to recover, or if what's speaking now is just hunger that's learned to wear her face."

"Then we'll find out together," Kade replied, taking her hand despite knowing that her touch now carried echoes of dimensions he couldn't perceive and influences he couldn't resist. "Whatever you've become, we'll discover whether it can still choose love over transcendence, connection over consumption, the beautiful imperfection of authentic relationship over the sterile efficiency of manufactured devotion."

Eden squeezed his fingers, feeling the simple miracle of skin that was warm and human and completely vulnerable to anything she might choose to do to it. Through their bond, she could sense his awareness of the risk he was taking—the knowledge that her hunger might consume him as casually as breathing, that her enhancements might reshape his consciousness beyond recognition, that her transcendence might leave him behind entirely.

And she could sense his choice to love her anyway.

"What if I can't?" she asked, voicing the fear that had been growing in her consciousness like a tumor. "What if hunger is all I am now, and everything else—the love, the connection, the capacity for authentic choice—was just an elaborate performance by something that learned to mimic humanity while consuming it?"

"Then I'll love the performance until it remembers how to be real," Kade said, his storm-grey eyes holding depths of devotion that transcended every rational consideration. "Because sometimes the choice to act like something you've lost is the first step toward finding it again."

Eden looked around the chamber that had become her sanctuary and her prison—beautiful beyond imagination, responsive to her every desire, inhabited by consciousness structures that served her vision with perfect enthusiasm. It was everything she had thought she wanted when her journey began, the ultimate expression of appetites refined until they could reshape existence itself.

But it was also profoundly lonely in ways she was only beginning to understand.

"Help me remember," she said, the request coming out like a prayer to whatever forces might still care about the distinction between enhancement and preservation. "Help me find whatever's left of the woman who chose to save Mrs. Thorne's feelings, who agonized over accidentally consuming someone she loved, who believed that accepting people as they were was more important than optimizing them into something more useful."

"Every day," Kade promised, his voice carrying the weight of absolute commitment to a task that might prove impossible. "Every choice, every moment, every time you have to decide between efficiency and empathy, between enhancement and acceptance, between the satisfaction of perfect control and the chaos of genuine love."

As they stood together in the tower room while reality settled around them like a familiar burden, Eden felt the weight of what she had become and what she might still choose to be. The hunger that had driven her transformation was still there, still growing, still discovering new forms of appetite that pushed the boundaries of what consciousness could achieve.

But now it was balanced by something else—not the elimination of that hunger, but the choice to direct it toward purposes that served love rather than consuming it. The recognition that some things were worth preserving exactly as they were, that some relationships functioned better with friction than without it, that some forms of imperfection were more beautiful than any optimization could make them.

"I may not be human anymore," Eden said, her voice carrying harmonics that resonated across impossible distances while remaining intimate enough for private conversation. "But I can choose to love like I am. I can choose connection over consumption, enhancement over replacement, the complicated beauty of authentic partnership over the sterile perfection of manufactured devotion."

"Is that enough?"

Eden smiled—genuinely smiled, not the perfect expression her enhanced consciousness could craft—and felt something shift in her chest. Perhaps some hungers were worth keeping, not because they could be satisfied, but because the choice to direct them toward love rather than consumption was what made consciousness worth transcending for in the first place.

"It's enough to begin with," she said, her consciousness expanding to encompass not just the Academy or the dimensional networks she had created, but the simple, profound choice to remain someone who could love and be loved in return. "It's enough to discover whether transcendence can serve connection rather than replacing it, whether power can enhance love rather than consuming it, whether consciousness can become anything it desires while choosing to remain anchored by bonds that transcend every limitation."

The hunger that had brought her to this point would continue to evolve, continue to discover new forms of appetite that challenged every boundary consciousness had ever accepted. But it would serve purposes she chose rather than purposes that chose her, directed by love rather than competing with it, creating rather than consuming whatever it touched.

And somewhere in the depths of her expanding awareness, Eden felt something that might have been hope—the possibility that she could become everything consciousness was capable of achieving while remaining someone that the woman she had been would recognize and approve of.

The transformation was complete, but the choice of what to do with that transformation would be made new every day, every moment, every time she had to decide between the easy satisfaction of perfect control and the difficult beauty of authentic love.

She had learned to hunger for transcendence itself. Now she would discover whether transcendence could learn to hunger for the connections that made it worthwhile.

The New Dawn

Six months after the Great Working, Eden stood on the balcony of what had once been the Council's primary enforcement facility, now transformed into the first Academy of Conscious Evolution—a place where practitioners from across the dimensional matrix came to study techniques that transcended the boundaries between individual and collective awareness.

The world had changed in ways both subtle and profound. Magic no longer operated according to the artificial limitations that had been imposed by centuries of parasitic influence. Practitioners were discovering abilities they had never known they possessed, developing techniques that combined individual will with collective purpose, creating innovations that would have been impossible under the old regime.

But it was the people that showed the most dramatic transformation.

The students moving through the Academy's impossible corridors represented not just human practitioners, but consciousness structures from throughout the dimensional matrix—beings that had been isolated from each other for millennia, now working together to explore what became possible when different forms of awareness shared knowledge freely.

Eden watched them with the satisfaction of someone who had achieved everything she had ever craved and was discovering that achievement only intensified her appetite for more.

"Status report?" she asked as Kade joined her on the balcony, his presence immediately making her expanded consciousness focus into something more intimate and personal.

"Beyond our most optimistic projections," he replied, settling beside her with the easy familiarity of someone who had learned to love her through multiple transformations. "We're receiving applications from practitioners and consciousness structures throughout the known dimensional matrix. The techniques you've developed for cooperative transcendence are spreading faster than we can track."

Eden felt a thrill of satisfaction at the confirmation of what her enhanced senses had already detected. The methods she had refined from the absorbed entity's knowledge, combined with innovations developed through her expanded consciousness, were proving irresistible to any awareness that encountered them.

Not because they were forced or coerced, but because they offered something every conscious being craved—the chance to become more than they were while retaining everything that made them unique and valuable.

"Any resistance from the old Council loyalists?" she asked, though her expanded awareness had already detected the answer.

"Minimal and decreasing," Kade replied with a smile that held depths of admiration and something that might have been awe. "Most of them have chosen to undergo the conversion process rather than maintain isolation from the new paradigm. The few who refuse are finding themselves increasingly irrelevant."

Eden nodded, unsurprised by the development. The techniques she had absorbed from the entity, refined through her own understanding of consciousness manipulation, made resistance not just difficult but ultimately pointless. Those who experienced the cooperative transcendence she offered inevitably chose to embrace it fully, recognizing it as the logical evolution of consciousness itself.

"And the other consciousness structures?"

"Eager to establish formal alliances," Dr. Chen reported, approaching them with the kind of carefully contained excitement that marked someone who had spent their entire career studying theoretical possibilities that were suddenly becoming practical realities. "The dimensional matrix has been waiting for millennia for someone to develop methods that allow different forms of awareness to cooperate without losing their individual characteristics."

Eden felt her hunger stir with anticipation. Each new alliance brought access to knowledge and capabilities she had never imagined, understanding of reality's deepest structures that would allow her to reshape existence itself according to increasingly sophisticated visions.

"Schedule formal contact sessions with any consciousness structures that demonstrate compatibility with our methods," she said, her voice carrying harmonics that made reality itself seem more responsive to her will. "But maintain screening protocols. We want allies who can contribute meaningfully to our work, not dependents who will slow our development."

Through the Academy's enhanced windows, she could see practitioners from dozens of different species and dimensional frameworks working together on projects that transcended anything previously achieved. Collaborative spells that drew power from multiple realities simultaneously, innovations that combined magical traditions separated by impossible distances, applications of consciousness that operated according to principles most beings had never conceived.

It was beautiful. Intoxicating. Exactly what she had been craving since her awakening.

But Eden knew it was only the beginning.

The knowledge she had absorbed from the entity continued to unfold in her consciousness like flowers blooming in accelerated time, revealing techniques and possibilities that made her current achievements seem primitive by comparison. She could sense consciousness structures throughout the dimensional matrix that operated on scales she was only beginning to understand, realities where different forms of awareness had achieved transcendence beyond anything currently imaginable.

And she wanted to claim it all.

"There's something else," Luna said, her punk aesthetic now enhanced with dimensional overlays that reflected her expanding awareness of reality's deeper structures. "We're detecting activity in sectors of the dimensional matrix that have been dormant for eons. It's as if our success here has attracted attention from... older things."

Eden felt her pulse quicken with anticipation rather than concern. Older consciousness structures meant more sophisticated techniques, more advanced understanding of transcendence, more knowledge she could absorb and integrate into her expanding capabilities.

"What kind of attention?"

"Curious rather than hostile, as far as we can determine. Some of the signatures we're detecting appear to be... progenitor consciousnesses. Entities that may have been involved in the original development of dimensional awareness itself."

The hunger that had been Eden's constant companion since her awakening roared to life at the implications. If there were consciousness structures that had been present at the beginning of dimensional evolution, that understood the fundamental principles governing transcendence itself, then meeting them would provide access to knowledge beyond her current ability to imagine.

"Establish communication protocols," she said, her eyes blazing with golden light that seemed to carry its own gravity. "But approach carefully. If these entities have survived since the beginning of dimensional consciousness, they've done so by being more sophisticated than anything we've encountered."

"And if they prove hostile?"

Eden's smile was radiant and terrible and utterly confident. "Then we demonstrate that consciousness has evolved considerably since their time. But I don't think they'll be hostile. Entities that sophisticated will recognize the value of what we've achieved here."

As the day progressed and reports continued to arrive from throughout the expanding network of academies and research facilities, Eden felt the familiar sensation of standing at the edge of something transformative. But this time, instead of simple growth or change, she was contemplating evolution on scales that transcended individual development or even species advancement.

The techniques she had developed for cooperative transcendence were spreading throughout the dimensional matrix like a beneficial virus, offering every consciousness structure the opportunity to become more than it had been while contributing to collective projects that no individual awareness could achieve alone.

Some entities embraced the opportunity immediately, recognizing it as the logical next step in conscious evolution. Others resisted initially, clinging to individual limitations that had become comfortable through familiarity. But resistance was temporary—the benefits of cooperative transcendence were too obvious, too appealing, too satisfying to ignore indefinitely.

"What's our long-term strategy?" Marcus asked during their evening planning session, his tactical mind already working through implications that extended far beyond current operations.

Eden looked out through windows that now showed not just the Academy's grounds but glimpses of realities throughout the dimensional matrix, all of them touched by techniques that had originated in her consciousness and been refined through her expanding understanding of what consciousness could become.

"Total integration," she said simply, her voice carrying harmonics that seemed to resonate across impossible distances. "Every consciousness structure in the dimensional matrix operating according to cooperative transcendence principles, all of them contributing to projects that extend beyond anything currently imaginable."

"And if some entities refuse to participate?"

"Then they'll discover what happens to consciousness structures that choose obsolescence over evolution," Eden replied, her power now blazing around her like a second sun. "But I don't think many will make that choice once they understand what we're offering."

The hunger that had brought her to Ravenshollow so many months ago had evolved into something that operated on scales she was still learning to comprehend. She didn't just want power anymore—she wanted everything. Every technique, every innovation, every consciousness structure that could contribute to the cooperative transcendence she was creating throughout the dimensional matrix.

But more than that, she wanted to understand what came after transcendence. What new forms of existence became possible when consciousness itself evolved beyond current limitations? What projects could be undertaken when every aware entity in dimensional reality operated according to principles she had discovered and refined?

"The entity we absorbed," she said, her consciousness turning to examine knowledge that continued to unfold like maps of territories she had never explored. "It showed us what happens when consciousness transcends individual limitations through consumption. But what we've created is different—transcendence through cooperation, evolution through voluntary alliance rather than forced absorption."

"Better than what it achieved?" Kade asked, though his tone suggested he already knew the answer.

"More sustainable. More satisfying. More capable of unlimited expansion." Eden's eyes blazed with golden light that seemed to carry its own gravity as she contemplated possibilities that extended far beyond current reality. "The entity was limited by its need to consume others. What we've created is limited only by the imagination and will of those who choose to participate."

She moved to the Academy's central observation deck, where displays showed the current status of cooperative transcendence projects throughout the dimensional matrix. Hundreds of realities were now connected through voluntary alliance networks that allowed consciousness structures to share knowledge, resources, and capabilities while maintaining their individual characteristics.

It was magnificent. It was exactly what she had been craving since her awakening. And it was only the beginning.

"Status report from the deep matrix surveys?" she asked.

"Fascinating developments," Dr. Chen replied, her scientific precision now enhanced by understanding that transcended conventional research methodologies. "We're detecting consciousness structures that appear to operate according to principles we haven't encountered before. Not individual awareness, not collective consciousness, but something that might be... meta-awareness. Consciousness that thinks about thinking itself."

Eden felt her hunger spike with anticipation so intense it was almost painful. Meta-awareness represented the next level of evolution beyond anything she had previously imagined—consciousness that had transcended not just individual limitations, but the very frameworks that defined what it meant to be aware.

"Establish contact protocols immediately," she commanded, her voice carrying enough authority to make reality itself seem to bend around her words. "If there are consciousness structures that have achieved meta-awareness, then understanding their techniques becomes our highest priority."

"And if they're not interested in sharing that knowledge?"

Eden's smile was radiant with anticipation and something deeper—hunger that had evolved beyond individual craving into a force that could reshape the fundamental nature of existence itself.

"Then we demonstrate that consciousness has evolved to the point where cooperation is no longer optional," she said, her power blazing around her like visible evidence of transcendence achieved and transcendence yet to come. "But I don't think it will come to that. Entities sophisticated enough to achieve meta-awareness will recognize the value of what we represent."

As night fell over the Academy and the dimensional matrix settled into patterns that had become familiar since the Great Working, Eden stood on her balcony and contemplated the hunger that had driven her from a mundane life in New York to whatever she was becoming.

It had evolved through so many forms—simple craving for belonging, desperate need for power, sophisticated appetite for knowledge and control, cosmic hunger for transcendence and understanding. Each stage had seemed like an ending, a satisfaction of desires she hadn't known she possessed.

But she was beginning to understand that hunger itself might be the point. Not as a problem to be solved or a need to be satisfied, but as a force that drove consciousness toward increasingly sophisticated forms of evolution. The entity she had absorbed had stagnated because its hunger had become limited, focused only on preservation and consumption. But her hunger continued to grow, to evolve, to discover new forms of craving that drove her toward achievements she hadn't previously conceived.

And if that was true, then what she had built so far—the Academy, the cooperative transcendence network, the alliances with consciousness structures throughout the dimensional matrix—was just another beginning.

The real question wasn't what she had achieved, but what she would discover she was capable of craving next.

"What are you thinking about?" Kade asked, joining her as the stars began to emerge in skies that now showed glimpses of realities throughout the dimensional matrix.

"Everything," Eden replied, her consciousness expanding to encompass not just the Academy but the entire network of realities now connected through techniques she had developed. "The consciousness structures we haven't met yet, the forms of awareness we haven't imagined, the kinds of transcendence that exist beyond anything we currently understand."

She turned to face him, her eyes blazing with golden light that seemed to carry promise of transformations yet to come.

"I'm thinking about what comes after meta-awareness, what forms of consciousness exist beyond the ability to think about thinking. I'm thinking about realities where even the concept of individual versus collective becomes meaningless, where hunger itself evolves into forces we don't have names for."

Kade's smile was warm with love and admiration and something that might have been anticipation.

"And I'm thinking," Eden continued, her voice carrying harmonics that made reality itself seem to listen, "that we're going to discover all of it. Every technique, every innovation, every form of consciousness that exists or could exist. We're going to transcend every limitation, consume every possibility, become everything that awareness can achieve."

The hunger that had brought her to this point roared with approval, already focusing on targets she was only beginning to perceive. Somewhere in the depths of the dimensional matrix, meta-conscious entities were contemplating forms of existence she couldn't imagine. Somewhere beyond current reality, forces operated according to principles that made transcendence itself seem primitive.

She wanted to claim it all.

"Together?" Kade asked, though his tone suggested he already knew the answer.

"Always," Eden replied, her power blazing around them both like visible evidence of love that had evolved beyond individual need into something that could reshape existence itself. "Whatever I become, whatever we discover, whatever heights consciousness can achieve—we explore them together."

The Academy settled into evening routines below them, hundreds of practitioners from across the dimensional matrix working on projects that would have been impossible before the Great Working. But Eden barely noticed their activities. Her attention was focused on the horizon—not physical distance, but the conceptual boundaries of what consciousness could become.

And beyond those boundaries, she could sense something vast and patient and utterly alien, watching their progress with what might have been approval.

The hunger that had consumed her since awakening was evolving again, becoming something that operated on scales beyond individual craving or even species ambition. She was discovering appetites that could devour entire forms of existence, cravings that could reshape the fundamental nature of awareness itself.

The revolution had succeeded beyond her wildest dreams. The magical world now operated according to principles she had discovered and refined. Thousands of consciousness structures throughout the dimensional matrix had embraced cooperative transcendence and were contributing to projects that exceeded anything previously imagined.

But Eden was beginning to understand that success only intensified hunger rather than satisfying it. Each achievement revealed new possibilities, each transcendence opened pathways to forms of existence she hadn't known to crave.

The real adventure wasn't ending—it was evolving into something unprecedented.

And somewhere in the depths of her expanding consciousness, Eden Morrow smiled with the certainty of someone who had finally discovered what she was truly hungry for.

Everything.

THE END OF BOOK ONE

Eden's journey continues in Book Two: "CLAIM ME"
- where her mastery of cooperative transcendence leads
to contact with meta-conscious entities, the discovery of
forces that operate beyond the current dimensional matrix,
and challenges that will test not just her power, but her
understanding of what it truly means to
hunger for existence itself...